DAVID BISHOP

Copyright © 2021 David Bishop

ISBN:

9798742995197

To David, Amy, April and Katy
for all your love and support.

FOREWORD

He had been running, in the dark. The worst kind of running, some might say. Running from and not to. And now, barring a miraculous turn of events he was likely dying. The worst kind of dying, some might say. Not that a young mind would acknowledge the existence of the ultimate fate, even though the first creeping fog of unconsciousness would be rolling in any time soon. Thrashing and kicking wildly, his airways naturally beginning to close to prevent the freezing water to penetrate his burning lungs, he fought to overcome the paralysing fear and shock which would only abet his demise. Hypoxic convulsions had already begun.

The earthy blackness of the stinking morass pulled at his clothes, their sodden weight conspiring against his floundering efforts to reach the unseen steep grassy bank of his undoing. It had lay like a trap to prove claim to his naivety. The moonless night sky and bare earth all merged as one, no lines or barriers to define water, earth or air. Vision became a worthless sense, disorientation dictated there was no up, nor down, no path for safety. Sinews stung with the groping efforts to avoid being sucked into the perishing hell, the foul mire of cloudy mud his sandalled feet had kicked up from the bottom filled his nostrils, stung his eyes and gritted his clenched mouth. Twice now he had felt the firm floor of what must have been a river or large pond, only to slip and plunge again into the clutches of the brain numbing murkiness devoid of any sense of the surface. The heavy tweed coat worn to protect his undernourished frame conspired with the peril to hang like a millstone, short trousers the only concession to movement in his limbs. Under the surface, there was almost a peace of muffled gurgling and bubbling where sound never penetrated. Breaking through again there was a chaos in his water filled ears of splashing, the desperate gasps for air, a primal bewailing.. 'Stay upright, stay upright!' His instincts screamed.

Voraciously heaving for precious oxygen, and treading the feculent, stygian waters, he silently pleaded for the unstable bottom to rise up and bring an end to this nightmare. A searing pain burned through his chest, leaden limbs slowed to a numbness, fingers were deadened with bitter cold. His deranged brain whirred in a motley jumble of self-pity and fear, but overriding all was anger. Anger of his own ignorance of succumbing to this strange deadly habitat. A bizarre day had contrived to end like this. It shouldn't have happened, needn't have...

CHAPTER ONE

One end of the twine was wrapped around his index finger, taut and eager. Anytime now, patience was key. Unconsciously he held his breath in anticipation. Doleful brown eyes focused, mouth dry, palms moist, heart beating faster. It never changed at this critical point, the adrenalin rush, the challenge to his skills.

Twenty yards away, a half-moon shaped net lay inconspicuously around a small heap of thistle and dandelion heads. A pair of outrageously plumaged Goldfinches flitted nervously nearby, fervent for the feast, wary of danger. A third hopped close by, summoning the nerve to join them, narrowly outside the nets range, he judged. The temptation was tormenting the kaleidoscope of red, gold and black birds and soon enough, the first one to succumb would reassure the others. Jerkily they scanned about, twisting this way and that to gain a complete overview, their tinker-bell song that of wind chimes in a breeze. The latecomer onto the pile of seeding heads tugged in a frenzy at the prize, settling the doubts of the pair who neared closer. Somewhere in the orchard an apple thudded to the ground, bounced once and then settled in the grass. As one they stopped feeding and froze, scanned some more, and continued on.

The low trees dripped lightly from an early morning shower. Hessian sacks brim full with cider apples a couple of which he used as covers, lay bulging against the gnarled trunks the harvest soon to be collected for processing.

Jem's knees were damp, his thick brown mop heavy with the moisture he had become oblivious to.

Thwack! He yanked the line and triggered the net to spring its hinge half flat over the unsuspecting Jewels. All three! Excitedly he rose and clumped his way in laceless boots through the damp grass to claim his feathered bounty with an exhalation of relief. On close inspection, however, the lopsided grin slightly waned. Whilst two birds lay under the net, immobile and helpless to their fate, the third lay under the metal rim of the nets edge, broken, dead. He had misjudged. He took it as a personal affront to his timing. On his knees again to the remaining booty, he lifted an old pair of stockings from around his broad neck, as a priest might deliver a blessing. Carefully feeding a large hand under the net, he gently extracted a bird, feeling its warmth in his palm and fed it headfirst into one leg of the nylons where once again it would be rendered motionless but unharmed. The other leg was already occupied by previously caught victims. When the task was complete, the lightly bulging hosiery was once again hung around his collar and tucked under his jacket in the fashion of a poacher. The tinker-bell song was silenced. It was time to pack up and return to the daily chores that began before dawn and ended after the onset of these early autumn evenings.

Doggedly he made the well-worn route through the sweet-scented orchard, and through a small thicket

2

that would lead him back to the farm and the resumption of his duties.

The morning chill failed to penetrate his everyday garb of a ragged pinstripe jacket and trousers, at odds with his surroundings and well-worn to a shine, cuffs and turn-ups were rapidly rising up the limbs of an ever-growing adolescent frame. A large head sat on already broad shoulders. Ill-kept hair covered a high forehead, under which a wide freckled nose and a thick lipped mouth with a rictus grin gave an overall slow-witted appearance. 'A face made up of leftovers' it had been said. In all, he resembled a neglected geranium or begonia that needed a tactful pruning, or at least, re-potting.

Misserly farm tended a small herd of beef cattle under the protection of a collection of barns, outbuildings, lean-tos and sheds, all in varying states of disrepair, often relying on each other for support like a group of inebriates tottering home. The more robust of the walls were constructed of cinder block or wooden rail sleepers, the farrago roofs of corrugated iron pan tiles, bitumen sheets or tarpaulin weighted down with old tyres. Windows, where there were any, were steel framed, more often filled with sackcloth than glass. Cast iron guttering, rusted and cracked, had filled with moss and debris over time, long since failing in their purpose. The quadrangle yard of which the buildings formed had disintegrated into an uneven spread of broken concrete, mud or oil sheen water, dependant on the fickleness of the drainage. The detritus that generations of unstable farming had resulted in lay scattered about in varying states of disrepair neglect and abandonment.

Rusting implements, unrecognisable from their dissection; a wheelless cart alongside cart-less wheels, engine casings, wood stacks, bales of ferocious wire and rusting oil drums, all contributed to an overall portrayal of impoverishment and indifference. The solid stone-built house that fronted the yard had fared little better. Its wooden windows allowed little light to penetrate, their peeled and blistered frames warped or shrunken, had long since made little use of their hinges. Odd tiles had slipped from the high-pitched roof and rested in the valleys.lead flashing flapped loosely from around the chimneys, where in spring Jackdaws nested to a raucous chacking. The old house faced a winding lane, a small stagnant brook separating the two. At its entrance, a sentry-like concrete plinth supported two battered milk churns that had not been whetted for some years. Over time, yields had shrunk to make the dairy herd unviable, a dwindling beef herd now the only defence from penury.

Four generations of the bottle lineage had scratched a living here and most had died here, save two young brothers who had perished far away in France in 1917. The third brother, Clem, a broken man with a broken body who had never sought, nor found a wife, was reaching his fiftieth year as custodian, along with his younger sister Grace. Time, mourning and ill health had soured him. A permanent frown had cut deep into a bony, liver spotted forehead, worn over sharp, moist black eyes, a hook nose, and paper-thin lips, all set on the complexion of an ageing apple. In his youth, a pitiful accident when trampled by a frenzied cow had pared his abilities, dulled his ambition and embittered his spirit. On the worst days, the ghosts of his beloved younger siblings came to taunt, bearing their gifts of guilt and shame. The pain of these visits confined him to bed more easily than any torment from his maimed frame. On such days save the juvenile efforts of Jem the beasts in the field were often left to fend for themselves. Sugar beet

4

lay to rot, peat lay uncut, and the wind was free to run amok in the idle yard, spinning straw in circles, banging barn doors and slamming old squeaky gates on rusty hinges.

Grace was of a somewhat lighter disposition though wracked with the fragility of her nerves, the simplicity of her mind leaving little room for deeper ponderings. More often, she would dart about skittishly about in her thin frame, with a birdlike tendency to jerkily look about, unable to settle on one task or even a thought, before another would interrupt and impair her ability to complete it. Her curly brown hair fought to be free from a permanently worn head scarf, occasionally escaping into a long twisting lock which would dangle in front of her prematurely ageing face, unattended for the day.

Her slender fingers would dance and settle on one chore, alight and settle on another, like a Tortoiseshell butterfly spoilt for Buddleia. All the while, she would be muttering inaudible ramblings under her breath with an almost imperceptible trembling of her rosy cheeked face. These unruly traits would often lead to pans and kettles to boil dry, the kitchen fire to expire and the kitchen tap to flood the flagstone floor. Bitter chiding from her brother would only accelerate her anxiety and serve to increase the calamitous incidents. Jem would accept his mother's weaknesses with forbearance, often foraging his own meals or fuelling the fire without comment.

The whole was set in a nondescript outpost of the Somerset levels, a peat rich, flat land that lay at the foot of the far-reaching Quantock and Polden Hills like a welcome mat. Scudding winds more often raced down their contours and across the moors, buffeting lapwing and snipe in their wake, sedge and willow bowed in obedience. Straight cut water ditches, or 'rhines' as they were known locally, had been fashioned by ancients in a grid-like pattern to irrigate the pasture and control flooding, hence allowing the 'summer settlers' year-round access to the land.

In times past, this had been the site that witnessed the last great battle on English soil, the bloody pitchfork rebellion, when a wilful mob of battle innocent labourers and herdsmen took up improvised arms against the Kings troops. Even now, an occasional musket ball or broken ramrod was regurgitated by the once blood-stained soil, as a reminder of the carnage suffered by the ill-fated roundheads.

Since Roman times men had kept their fires burning by toiling their long-bladed peat spades to extract the rich black soil. Brick towers, like ventilated termite mounds, were stacked in the fields to dry. Grass keeps and pasture rolled far into the distance, broken here and there by cider apple orchards, where Kingston Black and Sheepsnose hung heavily at this time, the liquid currency of these parts.

Where once the great King Alfred found refuge and planned his defeat of the Danish invaders, quietude had long since reigned, broken only by the lowing of cattle and the twitter of Skylarks tumbling from an endless sky. Somnolent and dry of ambition, it was left to do as it pleased, allowing time to be its master and apathy to be its slave.

CHAPTER TWO

On locking in unison like the legs of a stubborn donkey, the huge wheels of the locomotive skidded to an ear-screeching halt, unleashing a plume of smoke, fierce hissing steam and a token gesture of human freight that trickled warily from its carcass like fox clubs tentatively exiting their lair for the first time into the strange new world.

Terry Sharpe had inspected the meagre welcoming party through cynical young eyes. His reluctant gaze was cajoled from a breath tainted window and persuaded out onto the small station platform by a stout, competent women's voluntary servant as she had done four times already this long day. Mrs Irene Davy had bore the tiresome journey from Walthamstow alongside a thirty strong wide-eyed juvenile army with an equally stout and competent execution of her duties. Dispatching her charges at various stops on route with the help of colleagues, she had no intention of failing in this, her final terminus with the last of her liabilities

These were the leftovers. The unclaimed baggage, disregarded by potential new 'owners' and loaded onto the train again in ever dwindling numbers and enthusiasm. For some of the most brittle of them it had been too much. Damp eyes, damp pants. Like walking off the edge of the world, their known world anyway. Most had never experienced a train journey, the stuff of dreams with its departure, now the reality of arrival spun into a living torment. For the more brave, intrepid, or simply indifferent, it was the first tangible page in this bewildering comic book of war.

Each rigged out in unknown clothes, guided by unknowns to seek shelter, under an unknowns roof, for reasons unknown. The antithesis of peace and war held little regard for this particular brood, who thus far in their existence had tasted the bitter fruits of impoverishment, homelessness, or cruelty. Rejection was no more than another bruise or grazed knee.

Shapton village station, of no more consequence than an artery of a thinly spined vertebrae on which was conveyed the earthly fuel of these parts, was cast to the early, speckled dampness of a chill October evening. A thin pallid sun had surrendered behind distant blue hills as though it had seen quite enough for one day. A biting easterly wind chased along the single railway track and whipped around the diminutive flock like an invisible sheepdog, herding them together for protection. They circled the wagons too from a sudden burst of activity, busy chatter and advancement from a handful of curious villagers who had gathered to inspect the half dozen remnants of the venture. Their noise echoed from the station's wooden walls and soot blackened roof soffit, the bidding had begun. The arrivals were pushed, yanked, and spun around. Their chins were thrust upwards by calloused hands, while Mrs Davey waved her hands above her bonneted head, loudly beseeching for a semblance of order and restraint.

"Is-is this it?" Demanded one disgruntled man, a consoling arm wrapped around his young wife's shoulders.

"We wuz told there'd be babies!" Protested another middle-aged couple, who turned to leave the bidding for this batch to the others.

"Waste of time, two hours we bin 'ere," they shuffled toward the exit door, empty handed. Twin ginger headed boys who had been locked together in silence for the whole endeavour that morning were prized apart for scrutiny, their sudden howls of protest adding to the cacophony of commotion.

"Ain't none o' them got any bones for farmin'," grumbled an older man engulfed in a brown milking coat and wellington boots, seeking a candidate at the other end of the scale, though he had taken note of the pubescent frame of a twelve-year-old sulky girl with a solicitous vetting. Mrs Davey was busy defending herself against a barrage of hostility from dissatisfied locals who thought they had been duped. A porter who was wheeling a trolley constantly scattered the groups with an irritated 'mind your backs' aggrieved at the intrusion on his platform. Mild chaos ensued as the chatter was bandied into the evening air along with the pungent odours of urine and carbolic soap. Name tags hung around their necks like price labels, were examined as if to give some indication of character or potential trouble. An overweight pig farmers wife, her grubby headscarf wrapping her brown creased face, snatched at the hand of a twin and tugged him from his distressed brother.

"I'll take this un," she declared. A prospective custodian thought otherwise and grabbed his free hand ensuing a tug o' war.

"You don't split the 'andle from the bucket, you

apeth Doreen," she chided her neighbour and with a swift movement grabbed the other twin and presented herself to the relieved volunteer.

"Tweedledum an' Tweedledee 'ere, I'll take 'em both" she insisted with a no-nonsense approach.

"Gawd knows 'ow I'll tell 'em apart though. Reckon one of 'ee is goin' t'have a fringe cut off, probly you dum" she addressed one, lifting his cap. He had already linked his spare hand in reunion with his brother in assuagement. All the while, the huge iron horse continued to snort and wheeze its air and steam like it too was exhausted by the day's events. The porter insisted on his overly assiduous business, it was not that often he had a 'proper' train to deal with.

The boy, as he had done so before, attempted to distance himself from the melee, turning his coat collar over his ears and retreating in slow steps, as if melting into the background. His brown hemp attire bore the drab thread of pessimism, and the style of thrift that underlined the 'make good' consent of these times. His sullen eyes took in the dilapidated state of the neglected stop. Butter coloured paint flakes, teased by the wind, lifted from the wooden soffit and tumbled down, twisting and turning like autumn leaves that clogged the railway line and scattered the platform. The largest flake of which was the size of a half crown, he caught in his hand and crushed. Against the timber clad walls lucid rectangles enjoyed hitherto unknown daylight exposure, underlining the latest Whitehall directive for the removal of location signs, so each stop in turn became only that, a nameless place on a route-less journey. Wherever this place was, whatever identified it as unique, was yet to be discovered.

The time of the removal of all orientation markers reflected a period when the populous had reached a junction in its own future, each seeking a bearing in each other's eyes, a destiny an assurity of safe delivery from this unwanted excursion.

"Sharpe!" He was summoned from his reverie. His absence had been noted. A firm grip on his shoulder and he was propelled toward an imposingly tall Cleric, donned in a black trilby hat and full-length black frock coat with mud splatters around the hem. He peered down through small pince-nez that saddled his thin nose, fixing his glare on the boy as a kestrel might eye a vole. The unwilling victim fixed his own gaze on the deposits on the coat. With closer inspection it had collected burrs, fairy seeds and a multitude of cat hair. A timid face appeared from around the clergyman's rear. A heavily made-up face in a fur collared coat and veiled hat, that viewed him with suspicion, which became instantly mutual. Though only half exposed by her husband's shielding body, he could see she was smartly dressed in a pristine under-jacket and skirt with shiny black court shoes. Her make up reflected that of a practising young girl. Circular cheeks were smothered in rouge and bright red lipstick had been clumsily applied, so much so that it had tipped over the edge of her lips and revealed itself on her front teeth. A heavy cologne choked the air around her.

"This is Terry Sharpe," Mrs Davey stood behind the boy with a firm hand on each shoulder and offered the introductions.

"He understands a little better of today's purpose and being a little older, he will adapt to benefit any household," she then turned him toward her. For the first time he noticed a sprouting whisker on her chin.

"Terry, the Reverend and Mrs Garville have generously offered to accommodate you for the duration" she forced an encouraging smile. Of all of them only Mrs Davey looked pleased with the arrangement.

"Well, boy" the Reverend rocked on his heels and clasped his hands behind his back, unable to disguise his chagrin.

"You've no doubt acquired several more years than either my dear wife or I anticipated, but nevertheless a Christian duty cannot be denied. I daresay the lord will provide" the W.V.S woman nudged the boy into a response, only to receive an indifferent shrug.

"Mmm," mused the Cleric "popular rumour tells of impending shortages but food for thought we have a plenty" An air of dissatisfaction about the whole arrangement propelled Mrs Davey into expedient completion of the alliance, lest her good work be undone, and hastily finalised her notes before ushering the group through the station exit door.

They filed out with the frock coated clergyman to the fore and his thus far mute spouse followed behind, as seemed their natural order, to where three old model cars and a horse and cart had been parked in front of the station. Beside the first car, a green mud splattered Austin, the boy was ordered to wait while Mrs Garville had her passenger door ceremoniously opened for her. In the pause, the boy looked disconsolately around to where the dusk was settling quickly over open fields stretching as far as the eye could see, old dwellings few and far between. The day had revealed such vast tracks of nothingness, far beyond his imagination, a foreign country to his urban experience. There were no streets, traffic bustle of crowds, only emptiness. A green void. This hollow vacuum had finally claimed him, making all attempts of previous escapes from the clutches of strangers even more resentful. The journey had ended to its worse consequence.

The Reverend had returned from around the car and dropped his voice speaking almost confidentially though still firmly.

"Understand at once, boy" he began, inferring it was how he was to be addressed henceforth, "my wife is under considerable strain and suffers from a malady that demands the upmost peace and quietude. You will, therefore, be a stranger to her company as much as is possible, and I will not tolerate any form of distress on her part. Any contradiction of my expectancy will result in appropriate retribution. Do you follow?" His piercing stare bore into his reluctant guest. He opened the back door and gestured the boy in with a flick of his head.

Ushered into the back seat, Terry's olfactory senses were immediately struck by a concoction of dulcifying smells, not least the staleness of the reverends body odour and the sweet stickiness of his wife's perfume. That, combined with the nauseating redolence of tanned leather, snatched at his breath like a hand to his throat. Climbing behind the steering wheel without removing his hat, the Reverend patted his wife's gloved hand in sympathy, the gesture leaving no doubt as to their joint disappointment.

The sudden retching of such inhuman proportions from the rear seat begged the elders to turn and realise their worst fears. A mutual expression of astonishment turned to one of abject horror, paralysing the pair into non-action, in the time it took a muscle spasm of dramatic worth to eject the boys stomach contents along the back seat upholstery.

"Whhaaaghh!" Mrs Garville broke from her temporary mortification with a piteous wail, while her husband broke from his by attempting a wild lashing at the felon only to be frustrated by his seating position. Terry scrambled to the furthest point from the flailing and was spared when his door burst open, spilling him onto the road.

The resulting caterwauling of high-pitched howls and hollering, was enough to alert Mrs Davey who broke from another potential coupling to rush from the station exit. She was confronted by a vicious onslaught of un-Christian abuse from the seething Garville and wailings from his agonised wife who still had anything verbal to offer, other than the rendition of a suffering animal, her handkerchief only serving to redistribute her make-up in comic fashion. Seeking the cause of the commotion, the Reverend invited Mrs Davey to view the offending bile with a pointed finger at his leather work as evidence enough, to which she obliged and turned away much the paler.

"It-it hasn't been easy for any of them, you know," she recovered "it's been an awfully long day. These children have had a tough time you must understand — I'm sure once he's settled — ".

"Settled!" His eyes bulged wildly as he spat his full venom, his complexion turning a dangerous crimson.

"Settled!? That-that guttersnipe will no more settle in my home than the very devil himself! He is no more than filth; do you hear me madam? Filth! And you are not fit to undertake your duty in bringing these urchins here — are you listening?"

Mrs Davey had been distracted by the notable absence of the subject matter.

"Where is he?" She peered about into the developing darkness her charge had sunk into. Garville was in full flow, his wife reduced to a whimper of sniffles still holding her handkerchief over her nose, and still in her seat.

"Where's he gone?" Mrs Davey pleaded.

14

"Gone, is he? And a blessing too! Wherever he may cast his evil ways, may the Lord have mercy on any soul who may ever show him charity! They have all my sympathy!"

Mrs Davey continued to stare out into the empty night. Where had he ran? He knew nothing of the area, the terrain. What would happen to him out there in the dark?

CHAPTER THREE

"Right old state she was, all blubberin' away,
poor mare, sayin' how he shot 'himself in the barn and
what a mess it were. 'Course I thought she were sayin'
ee shat himself an offered t'take the hosepipe over t 'elp
'im clean up and for her to fetch some clean britches.
That's when I noticed she looked at I a bit funny. Could
see why when I went over, wouldn't be needen' his hat
again, never mind clean trousers. Blew his head clean off
'ee did, honest and truthful."

Rolo paused for effect to allow his audience a
reaction. Being a bearer and sometimes the subject, of
local gossip was a role he relished. He was just now
ending the news of a local farmer who has committed
suicide following an eviction order from the war
agricultural committee. He was satisfied to see his story
had had the desired effect on Grace, who exercised her
familiar horror at unwelcome news, and clasped a hand
to her mouth, shaking her head to release a curly
springing lock over her anguished face. Clem grunted,
doubted Rolo's part in the whole episode and continued
to stare at the fire moodily.

"I'm sayin' you need to keep your wits Clem,

16

there's this ministry chap goin' round causin' no end o' trouble." Clem spat in the fire contemptuously.

"I heard your truck was parked outside Ma French's all night t'uther night." He growled, to change the subject. Rolo looked affronted and widened his sparkling, merry eyes innocently.

"Now, who's been tellin' tales?" He defended "it so 'happens I was roddin' her flue. She gotta good fire goin' now. She ain't one for me, Gracie knows that don't 'ee girl? You'm the only one in me 'eart ain't that right?" Rolo pulled her weightless frame onto one knee while she, burdened with wet laundry, screeched coquettishly in false protest. They were sat in the flagstone kitchen, where rising vapour from the steaming copper boiler formed droplets on the yellow-brown stained ceiling. An adjoining parlour door ignored, the kitchen was the mainstay of the household where they ate, cooked, laundered, washed and excepting the presence of Rolo, mostly sat in silence. A heavy oak table with stout legs dominated the room with non-matching chairs, one of which was taken up by the visitor. A stone bath sink sat under the single window that looked out on the yard, a cast iron wooden mangle stood beside it. The black range at which Clam sat in his battered armchair, emitted a light grey fog as the peat smoke joined with the steam from the copper boiler.

Clem scowled at the antics whenever Rolo descended on them, his buoyant nature at odds with his own. To ignore the frivolities, he buried his attention in a letter he snatched from the table, though he had repeatedly read it several times since its arrival the previous day. His knees drawn up to the heat of the glow, his lips again followed the missive.

Jem had sat at the table munching on a thick slice of bread and dripping from a loaf that had scattered

17

much of its crumbs among the other general clutter it held. He was happily immersed in the company of the man he held in awe; his eyes fixated every nuance of expression from this character whose very presence would lighten the darkest room. Whose outrageous tales took him to a world so unlike his own, one of colour and amusement, and whose knowledge and wisdom made him divine.

By now Rolo was espousing in solemn tones to an enthralled Grace of how he had been nominated for the position of Mayor to Mendon, a market town some fifteen miles away, on the understanding that he find himself a suitable candidate to be Mayoress.

"I can see it all now Gracie, you in your finery, with everyone bowin and scrapin' to 'ee and' me all dashing an' handsome wi' me gold chains." The fretful woman blushed. Squirming she retracted herself from her tormentors' clutches and dumped the damp washing on the table, covering the loaf. She fetched a warming jug of cider from a pan on the range which she then passed to the grateful visitor with soap sudded arms, standing just close enough to his vicinity that he might be able to grab her again, if he chose.

No one could quite remember when Rolo first appeared in the area, nor much of his background, unless his endless and sometimes contradictory narratives were to be believed. Though his agricultural skills were undoubted, he spoke of years at sea and of being the bastard son of a local squire of whose inheritance he had been denied. He'd spoken of an errant wife, who had fled at the altar to pursue her dreams of becoming an actress, and whose subsequent success forbade him from revealing her name, lest it dented her rise. He even spoke of a spell of sheep farming in Australia, which ended when he was recalled by his Majesty's Government to help quell the Easter uprising in Ireland.

All these stories were regaled in such vivid detail, as to leave no doubt of their worth. His accent betrayed a mixture of dialectic traits, some educated tones, a light touch of West Country, with a tendency to drop aitches randomly. The only thing they were certain of, he was travelled, though his mode of transport was equally enigmatic. More commonly, he would favour a green brown Commer van, which he had inventively converted into a personalised abode. Besides a fold down bed, it contained a Rayburn cooker, complete with stovepipe chimney that poked through the roof, and small windows cut into either side with flowery print curtains on a wire. Small cupboard spaces contained his needs which seemed few, a drape separated the living space from the driver's cab. The jalopy was a familiar sight thereabouts, randomly parked with or without its owner, but more commonly in nearby woods, where he was known to keep a charcoal kiln. He was, however, known to emerge at any given destination on a pushbike and once, even horseback.

Today he was assumed to have arrived on foot, as no other mode of transport was visible, though from where or how far he had come would remain a mystery. Any form of enquiry was futile as he would parry it with a sly tap on the side of his bulbous, blue veined nose with threads like stilton cheese, and a knowing smirk.

He was of an indeterminate age. Certainly not old, with the fitness and strength of man in his prime. He bore black mutton chop whiskers on his rosy cheeks and dancing eyes that sparkled under an ever-present black leather trilby. His solid frame and barrel chest gave him the local respect his talents underlined. He wore a moleskin waistcoat over a collarless shirt habitually, a watch-chain stretched over his girth with a fob that was referred to like that of a busy man. Known and liked by all, he worked around the area and further afield, sometimes disappearing for weeks on end. Skilled at castrating bulls, harvesting, repairs - from buildings to relationships, the latter of which, he had occasionally been responsible for due to late nights at the Feathers, entertaining patrons with his rich tenor singing voice. The local women who fell under his charms were happy to oblige him with a washed shirt or hastily made meal. Rumours abounded.

Today he had arrived to de-horn some young bulls on a prearranged visit with Clem, who was finding his own strength waning by the day. For this labour it was wordlessly accepted he would be provided dinner, albeit one of Grace's spasmodic efforts, unburdened by cooking time or choice of content. A warming jug or two of cider would always compensate.

"Got some goldies for 'ee Rolo, nine all told!" Jem burst his news, unable to contain his delight any longer. Eager to reveal his offerings to his champion, he revelled in the intimacy of their personal contract and proudly wore a lopsided grin. To please Rolo was everything.

"So, it's business as usual is it Jem?" The man rested his china jug on the table and turned to the boy.

"Nine you say. You'll 'ave me skint you will. A tanner each was it? There's me a poor and honest man 'an you drainin' what little I got to keep body and soul together." His contrived despondency halted Jem until he recognised the makings of a smile from the generous lips.

"C'mon then, let's take a look," Jem took his last gulp of the bread and eagerly made for the back door. They made their way down the concrete steps and across the yard, Jem with his chest out and chin high, like the big bass drummer of a marching band. To share his private domain with Rolo reinforced their relationship in the boy's eyes. Never was he happier than in the company of his mentor.

The old boar shed stood at one end of the paddock, built of waist high cinder block on a concrete base. It was finished with solid timbers and heavy gauge wire mesh, over cut windows at either end, topped with a rusting corrugated roof. The last porcine had long been sacrificed for cuts and never replaced. Jem had claimed the disused shed as his very own, with the ever-growing collection of nets, traps, and rods he acquired under Rolo's tutelage.

He turned the stout door handle and pulled, allowing the daylight to chase ahead of him. Rolo stayed in the doorway, giving room for Jem to enter. High in one corner hung a battered canary cage, suspended by a large nail in which a cock bullfinch suddenly began to hop from perch to perch, almost in greeting.

These were precious times. The times it was just him and Rolo. The person that gave him worth. The oblique and terse comments of his father notwithstanding, on the odd occasion he spoke at all, along with vertiginous ramblings of his mother, made for a solitary existence.

Centre most of his sanctum, an old table filled the space, supporting among other detritus was a wire mesh box frame, a crude construction of his own making. A cage to keep his captives.

The boy stood mortified. Save two makeshift twig porches, it was empty. On its wire hinges, the door gaped open. All at once a heart stabbing, nausea-gripping dizziness of non-comprehension filled his head, but that came as nothing by comparison to the fierce burning wave of utter humiliation. It was not possible.

There were no Jewels to lay at the feet of his king, no gifts to offer his paragon to ensure his blind faith was recognised. A heavy consoling head on his shoulder felt like a patronising blow, the sound of Rolo's retreating footsteps broke the silence, each one a stab of the heart. He stared at the empty cage transfixed still, willing it not to be true, there would be no presentation as he had imagined, the reward, not the money, but the bestowal of gratitude from Rolo. He could think of no bigger sin than to let him down. A floating image of his call on the birds the previous day replayed as he remembered placing a handful of chickweed to the frantically active trophies to pacify them.

"I shut the door" he muttered to himself, over and over "I shut the door, I know it, I shut the door." A rank, black and tan mongrel of considerable size and age, paced along the outside kitchen wall, dragging a thin rusty chain. It was fiercely intent on rubbing its mange ridden flanks against the roughcast to find relief of its affliction, open sores exposed between its matted fur. A corridor of hair stuck to the sharp stone lay testament to its mania. On reaching the end of the wall's length, it would turn and repeat the process with the other flank, backward and forward in perpetuity like a sentry. Its obsession ignored the presence of Jem, who sat morosely on the lowest of the stone steps that accessed the kitchen door.

Across the yard, a crow leaned its scrawny black body from its purchase on a roof apex and screeched a loud mocking 'caw' that echoed in the emptiness. From the calf pens that adjoined the barn under the crow, came the mewing and shuffling of the bullocks, one of which had particularly appeared to have caught the attention of Rolo and his cheese wire by the sound of its protestations. Originally intending to offer his labours to help, as he always did with the man's work, the humiliation was complete in his own mind, his enthusiasm to be in Rolo's company dried up like the spittle in his mouth. Rolo's very presence now had become a punishment, a torment set to last for the rest of the day. As an extra mouth to feed, his mother would concoct a feast with zeal to appease his endless appetite, the inevitable cider would follow, as would the jollities of Rolo's humour which the boy was determined he would deny himself as self-flagellation for his blunder.

Bed, when it eventually came was a restless affair, determined to drag out his punishment. The windowpane rattled more than usual, toyed by a keen wind. The woolly fibered over blanket itched like niggling ants, even the old great coat that normally weighed with a comforting pressure, refused to stay put, slipping to the floor at intervals. But the image of the empty cage was the biggest culprit of his sleeplessness. The missing birds a mild irritant in comparison to the self-inflicted shame of appearing incompetent to Rolo, all playing their part, there was still something else. Something that had he not been consumed with ignominy may have been more in focus and demanding of the attention his peripheral vision dismissed. Something that did not belong. Increasingly he convinced himself he'd seen it but at the time it never consciously registered, or was it just a figment, just another tease to end the day? He forced himself to re-live the nadir and picture the empty cage, the aberration that he swore had lain on the floor at his feet. Irritated to the point of mulling whether to slip on a coat and confirm his suspicion and barely able to suppress the urge, a fitful night's sleep ensued, finally determined to re-examine his suspicion at first light.

CHAPTER FOUR

Arthur Bolsover-Cox steered his beloved shiny black Ford Poplar through unfamiliar winding lanes, blind bends and overgrown verges in a state of mild agitation. Potholes and manure-spread surfaces did nothing to soothe fear for his paintwork. High hedgerows on either flank afforded little view or assistance to the route of his latest port of call. It was as though the inhabitants of these parts had a deliberate rabbit warren-like existence to confound a stranger, with no demarcation lines to establish ownership or boundaries. Indeed, it seemed from his critical observance that most of the land and even properties he'd passed, had not been lay claim to throughout time with the degradation of neglect. How anyone made a living here was beyond him. Around another sharp bend he braked suddenly at the sight of an oncoming cow, its heavy teats swinging fit to burst. Was the damn thing left to wonder at will? As it neared too closely to the bodywork of his motor, he wound the window enough to emit a shoo! Shoo! Following up behind was a lad in a scruffy suit jacket oblivious to the vehicle, waving a stick idly with which he swished the heads off overgrowing thistles. The mud splattered animal brushed past an increasingly irate Arthur who did his best to scowl at the boy. The look he received in return cause him to retract his vehemence, the features enough to cause him discomfort, albeit from the safety of his seat. Never had he seen such an ugly boy, who hadn't even pulled a face at him. Another example of this inbreed territory, he dismissed. He crunched heavily on a peppermint to forestall the heartburn that had plagued him of late, giving license to his well-groomed, pencil thin moustache to dance lightly over thin pursed lips, his heavy jowls flushed below marble round eyes.

A long and quiescent career in the Ministry of Agriculture had until now secured him a rather padded position, to the extent of having his own nameplate, a proud item he had ordered and paid for himself from the local stationers and placed proudly on a shared desk in a shared office in the city of Bristol. Working hours demanded little more than addressing, cajoling and appeasing sub-committees, constant shuffling of mountainous paperwork and the occasional chastisement of subordinates, especially those who found amusement in causing mischief with his nameplate. Their enthusiasm to conquer the mountain would often lead Arthur at variance with his fellows who never grasped that a full in tray was a tribute to his workload and therefore his worth. Along with his presumptuous status had grown his girth, a consequence of the laconic lifestyle which at this present time left him unprepared for the current mission entrusted to him.

Abruptly seconded to these rural backwaters and into the newly formed county War Agricultural Executive Committee, a clunky title even by his bureaucratic learnings, he had found himself, or so he believed, in the front line. It was a division principally set up to ensure maximum food production in these uncertain times. Farmers and indeed any plot holders needed to be encouraged in the fullest yield of potatoes, flax, wheat, vegetables or whatever the department decided was appropriate to the soil. In this past few decades of casual existence potentially productive land, now much cherished, had been allowed to run to pasture, or simply neglect.

After the Great War had taken its toll on young and able men to continue in the traditions of their forebears, willingness had corroded like the machinery that lay about like casualties on a battlefield. Farming was in a state of inertia and needed to be stirred into action, reform was going to be a long gravel road were it not for the ultimate weighty stick the committee had to beat it with.

Non-compliance of vital food production for the war effort would ultimately result in the seizure of appropriate land, property appertaining to the same and the necessary evictions of occupiers with new recruitment to ensure maximum efficiency to this end. It had become Arthur's role to administrate these draconian measures on the inhabitants who failed to plough the fields and scatter the good seed on the land. Heaven forbid that any of these inconveniences should cause him any sleeplessness, after all, he understood perfectly well that rules were rules and by their very nature were bound to be adhered to. No, the largest cause of his dyspepsia had been in the explanation of these terms to those affected and whose subsequent reactions ranged from a total lack of comprehension to downright hostility. More than once physical threats had resulted in a speedy exit by the harbinger. His irritation with yet another wrong turn growing, he conceded defeat and pulled into a recess in the hedge which allowed a gateway into a field and consulted the map again. The damn farm did not want to be found, it seemed. Get it done and then he could return to the sanctuary of the office. He had had enough of these backwaters, he mused. Perhaps it was time for a little elbow tugging and ear bending to persuade his superiors to delegate the dubious honour of this role to lesser mortals while he pursued work more suited to his skills. To his left, he glanced through a gate

to a large acreage of tall growing brown spindles,
bending to and fro in the breeze, a dense leafless forest
of thin cane. Withy! Damn Withy! How typical. It was
almost an epitome of the crusade before him. What good
were baskets when the clots were growing no food to fill
them! He ran a manicured finger over the map once
more. Where was it? Where o' where was Misserly
farm?

CHAPTER FIVE

Jem pulled at the wet and weed draped rope hand over hand in a well-practised manner. The dull shine of a sketchy autumn sun was fast diluting into its buff backdrop. A small breeze rustled the reeds and chilled his face. Overhead, wheeling mallard curved their wings downward and dropped from varying directions in a sweeping survey before chancing touchdown in the largest of the ponds. The former clay pit at which he stood was by far the most likely for his purpose, a scattering of four of varying sizes and colouration owing to their multiformity of vegetation or stagnation. Set to the extreme east of Bottle land, the ponds were isolated from each other by a meandering grassy path that varied from one to four feet wide, either side dropping sharply into the steep muddy banks. Tall reeds and full rushes spilled over onto the footpaths made it precarious to gain a secure foothold. Occasionally on scorching summer days he would swim here. Somewhere a large black inner-tube which he sat in and paddled with his hands could be found, but these short-lived pastimes were few.

One time he was attracted by the noise of laughter and shrieks of mirth from a small group of young boys from the village who were diving and splashing naked in the celebration of their youth. He watched from behind a small tree, enjoying their frivolities until he was espied by one of them who raised the alarm. As one, they grabbed their clothes and ran off, shouting mild insults in their wake. He stepped from behind the tree and tried to utter a plea of re-assurance to stay, but no words came out. The crooked smile dried on his face. Imitating their antics proved a hollow exercise, there was only silence and emptiness.

At last, the willow basket broke through the wind ruffled surface, brown water noisily poured from each interweave like a sieve. It was shaped like a long thin vase with a slender neck behind a wide mouth. Dragging it onto the bank he then inspected the contents via a hole in the bulky belly of the trap. It revealed no more than the previous two, allowing a flicker of vexation to rise, the prospect of grilled eel for supper disappearing faster than the water spilling over his feet. Re-baiting with lugworm, he swung the basket in a large arc, watched it splash and sink quickly with the help of a weighty stone and checked the stake which anchored the rope. It was time to trek the half mile across the fields back to the farm. He was oblivious to the newly hatched craneflies rising from his heavy steps in the grass, his hands buried deep in pockets, and, more uncommonly, his large forehead was furrowed deep in thought.

Thus far the solitude of each day had never given him much thought for ponderance. It was a fact of life, like day and night, as much a part of the fabric as the farm itself. It would always be this way. His parents, and theirs before, had pushed their heads down through the challenges of each day, ceding to the demands of a life that by its nature could be cruel and unrewarding, like unbidden slaves not questioning of their duties and applying them with varying degrees of competence. Routine was the very axle of the task wheel that turned every day, and, barring any catastrophic events, carried out in the obedient muteness the isolation determined.

Unacquainted with everyday fellowship, the sporadic extremes of sorrow or joy, anger or merriment bothered him little. The pedestrian pace of routine offered sparse scope to flex emotions, and he adhered to the mindset of docile acceptance like the suckling cattle he tended. There was nothing here to rouse outrage except bad luck, which was futile, nothing to stir great rapture except good luck, which was scarce. There were days of non-utterance to a soul, save to acknowledge the begrudging curses of his father when he spoke at all, or accept the increasingly erratic ramblings of his mother.

The very nature of the Bottle detachment did nothing to curtail the wagging tongues of the hamlet on the event of the boys difficult and midwife less birth, on what was at the very least, a dubious parentage. Moreover, the lack of Grace's tendency to stray far from the farm could only be concluded in the worst possible speculation. Not that any of the whispers reached Jem's ears, who himself only knew the farm boundaries as his world and the adults as his parents.

Again, by the haphazard nature of his existence, he was allowed to fall through the gap in the floorboards with the local authorities when of schooling age, it was mutely considered by his parents that education was an unnecessary indulgence, as it had been for them.

Without a register of birth, neither baptised or Christened, with birthdays unacknowledged or declared with an inedible cake by Grace twice in the same year, he was neither despised, given affection, or treated cruelly, he was simply abided.

So, the Bottles grew again by one and continued in the time-honoured way they knew, and 'the boy' as he was regarded was absorbed into the framework of Misserly farm as any other of his lineage. It was a remoteness he knew as familiar as his oversize boots, but as he grew the boots would pinch and annoy. Right now, the only thing nagging away at him had left him in puzzlement all day. Following his restless sleep and making due haste to the pig shed, it was with a mixture of satisfaction that he'd been right, and confusion of how it got there. It had left him staring at an apple core at his feet. Someone had intruded. Broken in and let the birds out. Still, there were more questions than answers.

The keepers of the parish, though outwardly independent in their daily efforts, were nonetheless bound by the web that linked their existence, if not to flourish, then at least to scrape a livelihood. A loaned bull here, bales of hay there, bartered milk or cider in lieu of vegetables or free labour was the currency, with no requirement for bookkeeping or a tallyman minding due dates for recompense. Any departure from this unspoken accord would leave any transgressor paying a heavy price from the subsequent rumour mill that was entrusted as any newspaper of the day.

One such dark shadow had been cast over Clem Bottle who had the finger pointed at him for reneging on a consent to supply peat for potatoes from a neighbouring grower, and thereby distributed from all dealings except cold cash, of which there was little. In time, he was permeated back into the fold, lesson learnt. It was Grace, then a young flowering mediator, who trekked to the offended farmer to resolve the issue and curb a season of famine for potatoes successfully, although returning flushed and somewhere melancholy for a time.

Still there were the regular stock faces that dipped in and out of focus as the year took its cycle. In Spring and Autumn George Farrow, a raucous curmudgeon who bellowed in large tones, would trundle noisily down the lane on his David Brown tractor, its steel wheels announcing its imminent arrival, smoke bellowing and flywheel whirring, much to Jem's excitement. George would reap the hay and barley he grew on Bottle land leaving behind a percentage as rent. The agreement had lasted for some years until Clem, having been dissatisfied with his annual return, banished

George from future harvesting, and in not favouring himself or the land, it was left to run to seed.

In Autumn too, Mr Pittar, a florid, small-framed man with a pronounced limp that never curbed his jolly countenance, would arrive with his horse and cart to collect the cider apples, painstakingly picked by the family and collected into sacks. Two weeks later he would return with a bounty of the dry golden liquid in a large wooden barrel, the vintage of which would be discussed after copious tastings late into the evening, the adults in a rare state of equanimity which the boy relished. More than once Mr Pittar would be convalesced to the hay barn under a horse blanket to slumber until dawn, when he would vanish again until the following year.

Other infrequents would trespass the seclusion to buy peat, hawk oddments or simply to indulge in tittle tattle, the biggest culprit of which was Ma French, a wizened hawk-eyed harridan who brought bunches of meadowsweet and herbs, swearing by their relieving properties for various ailments. Her supposed knowledge of all goings on spilled from her toothless gums until exhausted of gossip, would send Grace into a frenzy with her insistent doom laden palm-reading.

The crumbling, fattened, burnt and sallow faces who appeared and vaporised like spirits on the ragged edges of Misserly were of little concern with the boys being, and soon he learned to dismiss them as a mild distraction.

Now everything paled into insignificance with his new preoccupation. More than that, it was growing to an obsession. Seemingly in a reverie in undertaking his days labours, his mind was in a fug like never before, brimming with the potential of his discovery. A primordial beast had stirred within and he knew not of the embryonic power it would hold. It rose from the very pit of his stomach until it pounded his heart, snatched his breath, filled his ears, and mussed his head. A hotchpotch of fear, excitement, anticipation, and angst, he knew not what, only that this unrecognised hollowness like a hunger must be satiated. The words of Rolo, while reciting his news update to his mother, at the time almost disregarded as his proclamations were wont to do, now came back to echo in his flux. It was of a runaway, a fruitless search, a young lad.

Chided over and again for the poor execution of his chores, the scoldings went unheededd. Peat blocks turned for drying collapsed in a shamble of stacking. Heifers stared longingly over a gate at their new pasture that was never opened. The mule got his hay, but his thirst went unquenched. Sucker calves got their water but failed to be reunited with their mothers and the milk they craved. Their baying complaints reverberated from the barn all day. Eggs went uncollected, the old mongrel got nothing.

His days rumination finally produced a strategy, and the first stage was about to be undertaken. That evening during a silent supper save the scraping of forks on plates, he bolted boiled potato and ham hock in record time as if it would encourage the others to do the same. The large potato smuggled onto the dying range went unnoticed by the elders, and whilst they prepared the rituals of an early retirement as they were inclined to do, he snatched it with pained fingers and secreted it into his jacket pocket. After some mental run-throughs and the frustration of their tedious delays, he feigned a last inspection of the calf barn, unsure the pen gate had been bolted securely. Willingly taking another curse at his folly, he picked a spare lantern from the table, and slunk out of the back door into the pitch evening, aiming straight for the pig shed, the bait warming his hand. Ceremoniously he placed the potato beside the goldfinch cage in obvious sight, stepped backward to admire his cunning and closed the door, sighing heavily. This was to be the proof of not only his suspicion, but his will, for it to be true. In the morning he would know for sure.

Walking back to the house gave him a prickle at his nape. Was he being watched?

The old cur beheld his return with a pitiful whimper in a desperate attempt at attention which went unheeded. He was about to incur his most restless night ever.

CHAPTER SIX

The summer sun bore down from a cobalt blue sky, not oppressively, but enough to emphasise its superiority. It was the god of all things and it wanted to flex its muscles. A warm current of air gently wafted the tall seeding grass into an uncoordinated dance of undulating ripples. Swallows skimmed, soared, and dived again, over the tops like terns over waves. A Yellowhammer broadcast its temperate song from a nearby telegraph pole. It was a perfect day.

They were all there, the four siblings, stripped to their singlets with the sapping heat. Grace sat behind them in her cart, playing with a corn dolly, whilst Clem, Will and little Alby toiling away, were jesting with one another, their skin shining with sweat. Secure in their common bond, father was a small distance ahead still donned in his waistcoat and cap, shirtsleeves rolled up his thick brown arms as a concession, scything back and forth like a pendulum right to left, right to left, barely pausing to wipe his dripping brow. The boys followed behind with their pitchforks, gathering the bleached harvest in piles to form ricks. Young Alby was playing the fool again, much to his father's ignorance, as he always did to win the acclaim of his brothers, the elder Clem admonishing him through suppressed giggles. It was a day that was set to go on forever and Clem was content that this time it would.

The farm was prospering then. With each year the willing young men grew stronger, and the work more easily managed. At supper time Will, the quieter more thoughtful of them, would pursue his argument around the kitchen table for investment in some of the new-fangled machinery that was changing the face of agriculture. Better use and drainage of the outer fields would realise their full potential and double their yields, the days of horse and cart were coming to an end, he'd insist. But father would have none of it. It was good enough for his father and his before. The two other youngsters would watch each debater like a tennis match, back and forth. Voices would be raised, the eventual agreement to differ good-naturedly forgotten until the next time Will broached the subject. It always began like this, perhaps this time, but no...

Father halted from his perpetual motions and stood upright to straighten his back, leaning on the scythe and called for the stone jug of cider ensconced in Grace's buggy. Heaven turned to hell in an instant. At once, rolling black clouds swamped the sunlight like huge waves on a small boat, plunging the field into cold obscurity. Swallows fell from the sky and crashed to the stubble screaming, stone dead. The catalyst had been father, who had turned to see Alby at his tomfoolery. His mellow face had become a distortion of wretched features, eyes bulging wildly, his mouth turned into a grotesque twisting snarl. He raged in a thick Germanic tongue. Charging at the boy, who stood still suddenly terrified, he took an almighty backward swing of his scythe and landed a merciless blow slicing Alby's head clean from his shoulders. Clem looked to see tears still running from the decapitated eyes. In a rage father cursed Will then, pursued him across the stubble and dispatched his head too in the same manner. Both heads rolled to Clem's feet and screamed for their elder brother to save Grace from the peril. Clem turned to run but the stubble had grown to its full height in an instant, holding him back like he was wading in chest high water. Father was closing in furious pursuit. His legs leadened, he readied for the blow, begging for mercy.

"What have you done?!" Father screamed at him, "what have you done?!" The scythe was raised for the fatal blow. Noooragghh!

He shot bolt upright, rattling the iron bedstead, eyes ablaze, panting heavily. Sweat had drenched his body and turned the bedsheets and heavy bolster pillow into a sour dampness. Tears ran down his sallow cheeks. He threw the coarse blanket aside and swung a leg out, dragging the impaired one to join it, and placed both feet on the bare floorboards, assuming a sitting position. A heavy silence prevailed, save for his rasping breath and the heartbeat of the ticking clock. His chest was tight, hands were trembling. A minute passed, then two. His own heartbeat subsided to almost its normal rate. By now he knew the process of recovery. There would be no more sleep tonight. Running shaking, thin fingers through diminishing damp grey hair, he wondered, had he screamed aloud? Had Grace heard him? She would not come, he knew. Not after that time. Not after that unforgivable time. His tortured mind ran through the images again, like the staccato pictures of a penny slot he once saw at Glastonbury fair. The nightmare was over again, and it was safe to reflect. It always began and finished in the same place. It was all Alby's fault he condemned. If only he hadn't made father mad, it could have been a blessed reunion. Not that you could be mad at Alby for long, such was his impish nature, the joker of the pack.

It was always good to see them again, enjoy their company. The way it was before the empty void when they left, the hollowness of the heart. Almost worth the pain, the condemnation of father, the fear of the scythe. He almost cursed the youngster again for the irrepressible spirit that undid it all. Restless, naive and adventurous, the daily toil never enough to burn his energy, it was he who persuaded the sober and thoughtful Will to join up too. Will, so stoic for his years, was happy in his own company creating things, improvised tooling and the like, the more intricate the better. Quietly for days he listened to Alby's insistent campaign to enlist, albeit he was barely of age. One night at the kitchen table on completing the repairs to a broken paraffin lamp, he laid down his tools and looked down at the would-be soldier. Alright, he had said quietly. I will come with you. Just to keep an eye on you. They would only be gone a year they said, look after Gracie.

He stayed out in the field the day they left. He could not bear to see their receding backs. On returning to the house later, he found his little sister sobbing into her folded thin, soft arms at the kitchen table. Father newly buried, mother before him, now the boys. He closed the images.

And now, irony of ironies, history of all the follies of mankind, this was surely the ultimate.

Had the boys survived the war, they would have been seasoned men now, able to witness this new conflict. How would they have judged this catastrophe? Would they have been as eager to heed the call to arms, naively blundering in as though their efforts would swing the balance? To bid him farewell once more, leaving him behind with the young and old, the women, the frail, and all the others of no fighting worth?

This time around he kept himself largely ignorant of the gathering clouds of fire and steel that shaded the buttercups and daises of England. Purposely oblivious to the news of dogfights screaming over southern skies, blind to the cities ablaze, the bombed-out homes turned to rubble, or left half exposed like dolls houses complete with furniture. The wireless Will had painstakingly fashioned over many nights, lay unbidden

in the parlour since the day the terrible news came. He
squeezed out the last of the tears from his crinkled eyes
and lashed out with his good foot at the half filled
chamberpot, sending it skidding across the floorboards
where it upended and shivered to a stop in a hollow
clatter. What could this war do to him that hadn't already
been done? He was dead anyway, he decided.

CHAPTER SEVEN

Jem was working himself into a fervour. An invisible thread had turned into a tangible cord, and he deigned himself the puppeteer who pulled the strings. His thought process was gathering momentum and careering like a runaway cart.

For five painstaking evenings, in the twilight of a hundred nocturnal watching eyes, he had smuggled morsels to the pig shed and joyously found them gone the next morning. But even then, the punishing dread that the offerings would be unbidden, and the cord broken, was becoming too much to bear. That the quarry would move on for whatever reason and be lost forever, a torturing prospect. The union had been made. This had already become one of the most important junctures in his life, in his mind. But from the weakened position of a subservient to the whims of another as he saw it, he needed to take control of the situation. And so, his cock-eyed plan was formed in the only way he knew. It was time to pull the string.

But this was no rook nor rabbit for the pot, nor songbird for the sixpences he had nothing to buy with. His urgency of possession of this prize made him oblivious to the consequences. With sober reasoning it was decided that the key to the success of any catch was the over confidence — or desperation of the intended victim. This had to be done, and quickly, before the bird took flight.

In the slow afternoon of the day, when the farm took its toll, he indulged in some deep foraging among the oddments of hardware that lay undisturbed for years, strewn about the barns until he unearthed a hefty return spring of the type that would naturally shut a gate or a door, in much need of lubrication. A broken chest of drawers in the hay store served as a makeshift tool chest and from here he retrieved a hammer, a screwdriver, and some loose screws. Avoiding the yard itself so as not to be side-tracked by an elder, he scouted back and forth through the maze. The plan had to be set up for that very night, if for nothing else than his bursting expectation.

Sometime later Jem stood back to admire his handiwork with a mixture of satisfaction and a glimmer of doubt. There was no going back on this. In his eagerness to secure the most cherished prize of all, he hadn't considered the consequences of his actions, the reaction of the potential captive.

The spring had been duly affixed to the solid pig shed door at one end and the door jamb at the other, the door then itself removed of its inner handle. The thick gauged mesh originally cemented into the cut-out window frames at either end was tested and shaken for its endurance. With an inspection of the solid walls and sturdy roof he was finally satisfied the most bizarre trap he would ever construct was fit for purpose. It only left for the hours ahead to dwindle away like a tortuous sentence for his barely believable hopes.

He hardly had time for the self-congratulation of his artfulness before the hubbub of raised voices from the yard inserted a distraction. With the door slamming gratifyingly shut behind him, he ferreted back a through the barns and out into the yard trying to bear an innocent air.

The distraction came in the form of the local

constabulary, or, more specifically, of one constable Butcher who strode across the yard trying to avoid puddles and cowpats whilst addressing Grace from over his shoulder as she trotted behind trying to keep pace, wringing her hands in her apron. Known more by his reputation than his presence, rumour held of an earlier demotion that caused him to vent his mettle as tight as his tunic. Stray cattle, a stolen pushbike, and drunk in charge of a horse, were not the issues to inspire a still ambitious lawman who swore by the dictum that everyone had something to hide.

His height was exaggerated by the pointed helmet, secured by a tight strap anchored to his chin which made it wobble as he spoke his clipped tones.

"Anything unusual, anything at all?" His interrogation seemed limited, demanding from the fraught woman a different answer to the same previously asked question. She shook her head in worriment. His cold, blue eyes glanced around at the dispirited state of the buildings and virtually dismissed them at once as any form of refuge. Clem had stood at the kitchen window, keen to observe but determined not to be involved. The constable's survey settled on Jem, who rushed from the paddock to make himself seen.

"You," he said bluntly. "You seen anything unusual, any strangers?" The boy joined his mother's side and gave a negative shrug. Momentarily drawn by the boy's irregular features, the policeman dragged his eyes away and took slow steps towards the barns, hands behind his back, deciding on a cursory inspection. Grace looked terrified at Jem as they stood in the wake of the brusque intruder. As he disappeared from view entering the first outbuilding, Jem fought an urge to follow. Soon enough though, he emerged back into the daylight after a token scouting, brushing real or imaginary dust and cobwebs from each arm in turn. It seemed any further search would be hampered by the threat to his immaculate uniform.

"And that," he re-joined them, casting his eyes over a low separate shed away from the others, still dusting down his tunic. "What's that, over there?" His accusatory tones unchanging. Jem followed his gaze.

"Boar shed." That the shed had long since neglected to house any porcine for some years, he failed to elaborate, but it was enough to satisfy the officer who was less than enthusiastic of the animals.

"Hhrrmm" he cleared his throat. "Well, if you see anything unusual or any strangers, you must report it immediately, is that clear?" He had concluded the mental capacity of the two incumbents was deserving of his mantra. They both nodded, though Grace's head was quivering from side to side concurrently. Looking down at his shiny black brogues which had collected an amount of dubious deposits around the edges, he turned and marched purposefully, retracing his entrance barring one or two sidesteps, still wearing his bicycle clips. They watched him skirt around the house and down onto the lane where presumably he would be reunited with his bicycle. By now Grace was trembling uncontrollably, and she looked at Jem, who was already her own height, for reassurance, or at least some form of explanation.

"Is-is-it—" she tried to force the word. Jem looked at her tortured face and finished for her.

"Germans?" He prompted. "Yeah ma — Germans."

Now the urgency to complete the plan was total. As he took his own scan across the myriad of barns, a nervous thrill ran down his spine. Was he somewhere in there at this very moment, the 'German?' Holed up, waiting to break cover under darkness? The suspense was almost unbearable. It was only left to fill the void of what threatened to be a seemingly endless few hours of daylight before the culmination of what was by now an obsession, the visit of the policeman only serving to fuel the fire. The pony's care, the husbandry of the cattle, even normally mundane chores became a groaning

43

weight of pressure, a stifling obstacle to his purpose.

Some days earlier a calf had been born, a welcome bonus to Misserly, under a difficult birth to its mother who was dangerously ill, an unbearable loss. Under Rolo's guidance Jem had hand fed the strikingly handsome newcomer that boasted four white socks and an otherwise complete rich red brown coat. He allowed a rare fondness when it began to mew for him on sight. The cow had thankfully recovered quickly, and now was a good time to reunite them and re-join them to the herd at lower field, for the last of grazing before indoor winter incarceration. An escape from his agony. With a rope halter around the cows neck she was led gently from her stall, out across the yard through the paddock, and down to the field, occasionally turning her head to check the calf was trotting loyally behind, while he looked back at the pig shed in anxiety.

In the dull glow of a paraffin lamp in the early evening, he shared a supper of over salted chitterlings and bread with his mother in habitual silence, Clem already having retired early with little appetite. In the unforgiving light she looked aged well beyond her years. The days travails of the intimidating constable's arrival had taken its toll on her fragile nerves and it was with some ease the boy was able to surreptitiously half-fill his share into some paper on his lap and secrete it into his jacket pocket once again. Painfully fighting his own trepidation, he muttered an excuse to use the privy before nightfall and rose to head out the back door — to what he had no idea.

Owing to Graces strain to concoct the meal, it was much later than he planned. October was giving way to its chilly heir with already surrendered daylight as he descended the concrete steps. The old cur, roused by the sound stretched at the full length of its chain tether in the hope of an attentive scrap. It was to be disappointed. A half-moon picked out the silhouette of roof lines, some horizontal, some apex guiding him off to the right and away to the intended structure. Nothing stirred. Only his own footsteps broke the silence.

Slam! The sound cracked the air like a rifle shot. Momentarily rooted, heart bursting through his ribs he dare not believe it. The door! It was the door! It had worked! Or had it? When finally able to force movement in jelly-like legs, dizzy with expectation, he ran across the paddock and reached the pig shed in a state of quaking fearfulness.

The thunderous noise from within left no doubt the offending door was taking a barrage of blows, kicks and guttural curses, filling the night air with a calamitous racket. The distance from the farmhouse made the uproar no cause for concern but the bitter anger that came with it was.

The outrageous success of his scheme was beyond belief, but any self-congratulation was tempered by the cacophony that clouded all reasonable logic of what to do next. At first, he could only uselessly wave his hands and make loud shushing pleas over the bedlam in a pathetic attempt to subdue his prisoner. But the howls of protest continued unabated. Rising to a panic Jem ran around the corner to a grille window, stumbling over rough ground, his heart beating outrageously. He pressed his face to peer into the dark void and instantly jerked back into shock.

A snarling, spitting feral face leapt at the wire, claw like talons gripping and shaking the firm base furiously. The jailer tripped and fell on his backside, looking up at the beast he had captured. White eyes pierced through a grime laden skin, hair a tangle of dirt and debris. Emitting a low guttural growl through blackened teeth and lips, the captive kept up a pandemonium of protests. Horror stricken, Jem scrambled up and ran around to the door again, the image still burning of what he had witnessed. The door was the only barrier between him and the seemingly half-human, dare he open it? Not least of his concern was his own safety against this ferocious force of anger. The banging and commotion continued vociferously. It was out of control. This wasn't how it was meant to be. All the previous daydreaming and speculation never contemplated such a disastrous outcome as this. He mentally begged for the commotion to end and his capture to realise his good intentions, but there was no way to explain his motives to the crazed boy, if that's who it was? He recalled the size of him through the grille, smaller than himself despite the murderous actions.

To catch a wild beast was one thing, to tame it into submission quite another. Now he began to berate himself, to what had he naively expected? A subdued, quiescent serf, grateful for his interloping? In truth he supposed yes, his musing had drawn a picture of a companion who was forever in debt to Jems prompt interference.

Now he wanted to run, far and fast. Take it all back. Have everything how it was, however much the newly found urge to connect with another of his own peer group pressed his conscience. Forget the newfound hunger to fill the void.

But still, the invisible thread would not let go. If he panicked and backed out now, there would never be another chance. An arm's length away was the previously unrecognised need, it only needed to be managed. It was a matter of breaking the colt. Once it realised Jem was not a threat and meant no harm to him, all would be fine. He had to make him understand. His own actions had been clumsy, he could see that now, however full of good intent, and it had all gone horribly wrong. His intentions misunderstood, he needed to make amends and explain himself. Then they could begin.

The noise stopped. Nothing. No banging, crashing. Not even heavy breathing bar Jems own. What had seemed an unstoppable attack of unbearable proportions had abated just as quickly. What was happening? A minute passed. Silence grew to become an offence to the ears as much as its opposite. It told him nothing. He pressed an ear to the door. Closer now than ever. A piece of wood between them, separating him from the instinctive affinity of his obsession. Surely not. It couldn't be that simple. The words came out in a trembling croak.

"Lo? Lo in there? — y-you alright?" He had spoken, made contact. A stranger desperate to befriend. The only apple on the tree to sate his hunger. No reply. Moments weighed heavily; his own heart still thumped wildly. "Lo?" Nothing. The state of affairs had swallowed him whole, he was out of his depth. Rolo would know what to do, but there was only himself and his urge to retrieve the situation. With a trembling hand, he reached for the door handle and began a gradual downturn, almost nauseous with apprehension, loathed to meet that fervid face once more. Very slowly, with the resistance of the spring, he began to pull the door open.

Crash! The full force of the door smashed into his face sending him sprawling to the earth. A flailing phantom flew out and over his prostrate body screeching devil curses and stole away into the gloom before his senses gathered to realise what had occurred. Groggily he sat up, feeling the stinging smart of his nose. A trickle of blood, little more. The fog of the events that began to reveal themselves on the carousel slowed. There was the door, like a punch in the head, the figure, the speed of which offered no shape or form, running footsteps fading. He focused on the door before him, slammed shut again, on an empty space. He was gone. Frightened off by the crass tactics. It wasn't to be, and he was only fooling himself it ever could be. A silly notion of taming someone to be compliant as a pet at his own behest, like one of the birds. Subdued as they became, they too would bid for freedom at the first glimpse of opportunity. Did he really expect a passive submission to this great blundering attempt at filling the solitary vacuum, the hole he had stood at the edge of?

The bewildered boy gathered himself to his feet and pulled the door open again, staring into the darkness of the shed. Only minutes before, it had held what was now a mere fantasy, there was nothing tangible here now only the certainty of carrying on in the way he always had done, with his isolated amusements. He stood back and released the door once more, allowing it to slam shut, almost symbolically, and trudged back to the house, each step weighing more heavily with the incongruity of the outward journey. Hands in pockets, the weight of the offering began to rankle. He lobbed it at the cur.

CHAPTER EIGHT

In her childhood the generous age gap between Grace and her two elder brothers afforded her a natural protection and dotage which she returned with boundless affection. Their father's fatal heart attack left her with dim and ever fading memories of a quiet but solid man, intent on edifying the boys into the farm traditions, whilst assuming her domestic instincts were innate as a female.

The terminal downward spiral of her mother's wellbeing soon after her birth left no memory by its nature, but the boys often said it was uncanny how she came to make and wear her own lavender water, just as her mother had.

Consequently, she was often left in charge of her siblings, who, whilst discharging their duties, often towed her around in a box on wheels with a string pulley fashioned by Will. She was soon to discover she could induce fits of laughter from an audience by emitting a high-pitched hum which quavered tremulously over the rough ground, with the vibration. From whichever precarious position she was placed and ordered to sit still, she would look on the boys in admiration. Thus, they grew as tight as young thrushes in a nest. Inevitable squabbles were refereed by the non-participants and judgement passed accordingly.

With the bombshell of the loss of the anchor their father was, the boys were driven from their comfort of youth and turned into men overnight. There was little time for grief and self-pity with the toil the farm demanded. Each played their part and for hers, Grace adopted a motherly role as best she could, tending her brothers needs with domestic zeal, albeit without the tutelage to hone her skills. And as she flowered, in misplaced loyalty they were quick to denounce any potential suitors for their sister, though none could be remembered specifically. If she were but to know it, these would be the best times of her life.

That this state of affairs would be accepted as the status quo and perpetuate without further loss or gain to the Bottle headcount, was never given daylight until the fateful day Albs exercised his newfound manhood with a lust for adventure.

At the battered old table where she now sat, glimpses of the past would break through the fog of memory, no more so than here, where in times past they would gather for meals and banter that would spill and bubble over like a rich rabbit stew. Where Will would take apart clocks to understand their workings or fiddle with his handmade crystal wireless set that fizzed and crackled and spewed strange foreign tongues or perfectly enunciated voices in sombre tones. And the music, that was the best of all. Then they would dance around the table comically to shrieks of laughter. Where Clem would draw up plans for future farm work and Alby would fidget and gabble excitedly about something that had stirred his curiosity. The battered old table that had soaked up her tears the day the patriots left. The table where now sat a bitter Clem. Aged, almost without resolve to continue, loathed to be summoned from his bed, wrapped in a heavy shawl over his nightshirt, unshaven and watery eyed despite the noon hour. The cause of the disturbance had been an unwelcome visitor as most were, even more so that this was a stiff collared stranger who emanated the cold detachment of officialdom. He sat uncomfortably clutching a brown, leather briefcase protectively to his chest, like a shield with one hand, and solemnly reading from a prepared statement with the other.

Arthur Bolsover-Cox, despite his professional countenance in discharging his business, began to feel most uncomfortable. It was an inauspicious start. Finally able to locate the farm and failing to receive a reply at the front door, which frankly looked as though it hadn't been opened in years judging by the ivy that claimed it on its upward journey, he was forced to traipse to the rear. This immediately put him at a disadvantage, trespassing into the unknown and further still from the sanctuary of his beloved ford popular should the need arise. At the rear he found the back door at the top of a small flight of steps owing to differing land gradient, at the bottom of which he fearfully encountered what looked like a hell-dog, though passive enough it stank like death. A quick glance about the yard and its dilapidated state confirmed his mission.

The initial conducting of affairs with this peculiar woman occupant, who he soon realised had no conception of his purpose, proved barren until she was forced to summon this bedraggled old man who looked like a hermit. At least the growing anger in his reddened eyes showed he understood the implications of Arthur's carefully chosen sermon and he hoped to dispense his duties quickly and depart. He continued.

"My committee, having completed a thorough survey of said boundaries, and finding them not having been run efficiently for food production under the Cultivation of Lands Act of 1939, have therefore recommended to requisition twenty-five acres of said land for food production…" Grace was staring at her brother for a facial gesture to interpret the stranger's words, fearful of what she saw. "…and furthermore, to drain eight acres south of pasture to cultivate root vegetables…" Clem was beginning to seethe "and to take possession of all buildings, dwellings, appropriate machinery and livestock thereof —"

Clem leapt from his chair, his shawl slipping to the floor, and banged his bony fist on the table so forcefully the milk jug spilled some of its contents. Grace jerked in shock. Arthur reeled back startled.

"Never! You hear? Never! This is Bottle land!" He shook in fury, eyes blazing, spittle dribbled down his stubbled chin, his face blackened with strain. Arthur tried to compose himself but began to rise from the table sensing the situation was about to deteriorate.

"I'm afraid Mr Bottle the committee will —"

"Get out! Get out!" Clem screamed. Grace began to cry. The ministry man needed no encouragement to take his leave and backed towards his exit, still clutching his shiny bulwark high to his cheek.

"You will be hearing from the ministry in due course, and I suggest —" Smash! The milk jug was hurled in his general direction and exploded in small fragments against the wall behind him, remnants of its contents running down in rivulets. Leaning across the table Clem was still furious.

"Don't never set foot yer again 'ear me? War effort? Be tryin' t' tell oi about war effort? Well, we give 'alf a family for the war effort 'afore. Ain't tha' enough? Get out now!" He spat. Grace had put her hands over her ears and rocked slightly.

Bolsover-Cox tried to utter his legal position while fumbling with the door and keeping a wary eye for more missiles. As he exited the steps, the door was slammed behind him, a rusty horseshoe lost a tack and swung ends downwards pointing, the kismet sign of bad luck. The cur gave a low growl. He rued having not driven into the yard rather than parking a distance not suited for his safety, making a mental note to be more astute next time. Hurrrmmph, next time indeed. He really must speak to his superiors at the first opportunity, this was work for a younger man.

If the full implications of the visitor's purpose were lost on a non plussed Grace, the choleric eruption of her brother's temper was enough for her to realise the gravity of the situation. She shook uncontrollably as Clem gathered his fallen shawl from the floor and left to retire to bed once more, offering his sister no comfort. She stared at the document left on the table. It carried the same official crest as one Clem had been studying some days before and though she was able to read a little, the official terminology was beyond her. Once again, the table that had long lost its varnish soaked up her tears.

Jem had been oblivious to the episode, having lost himself in his own melancholy. October was disappearing with the surrendering hours of daylight at either end and reducing his workload, which with the increasing absence of his father, was undertaken without preamble. Reluctantly entering the pig barn again, he had taken the Cock Bullfinch out across the fields to escape the farm and his failures. The hours spent in pursuit of the songbirds were becoming a restorative, filling the surplus hours once dreamily reserved for companionship.

Sometime before, Rolo had shown him a picture in a book and challenged him to build a box trap to lure finches. As ever, eager to please, he painstakingly produced a carefully constructed affair, resembling the dimensions of a shoe box. It was crafted from half inch wooden battens with cut up bicycle wheel spokes as cage bars, the whole split into three equal sections. The decoy or call bird was confined to the middle, where it innocently attracted the attention of its fellow species with its dulcet notes. The end compartments were open topped with a hinged door, an extended support notched onto a lower perch, with sunflower seeds or seasonal berries scattered on the floor. When the prey espied the food, it would land onto the perch, knocking the drop door above and be captured unharmed. Whereas the goldfinches were ground feeding birds, the shy bullfinches were reliant on seasonal berries and buds of hedgerows, food being the common lure to all species.

A grey wash hung over the late morning sky, though rain looked unlikely. The small field of his choosing was surrounded by high rambling hedgerows of blackthorn and wild honeysuckle to suit his purpose, the box trap settled onto a high shelf in one of the larger bushes. He crouched into a gap in the undergrowth some yards away, within sight of the 'bully' which was emitting its soft 'peep' call, unwittingly luring a fellow specimen to join it. Occasionally it would fall silent, and Jem would imitate the call with a practised whistle of his own to encourage it further.

Inevitably as he waited, the pig shed incident tormented his mind over and again, desperate to imagine a different outcome to his folly, berating how crude his actions had been. He struggled to remember what he had seen of the boy, shorter than himself, probably younger then, wiry but with the air of fury that spilled over to cloud the picture. Slowly the mists of his memory cleared to separate wish from fact. He began to see. The call bird, in undertaking its duties in ignorance was still loathed to be trapped, however regular its food supply, however safe from predators and harsh weather, however much its needs were catered, it was against all its instincts to be confined.

Of course, the boy was crazed. Probably scared to death at being caught as much as the birds flapped wildly at their initial incarceration. As far as he knew, the boy had been in hiding for nearly a week with only Jem's meagre rations to sustain him, cold, unwashed, obviously. a stranger to these parts. But what had he run from, and why? Something that was worse than skulking like a fox in the blackness for refuge, that he couldn't reveal himself for fear of capture. To top it all Jem had unwittingly forced entrapment which was the worst thing he could have done, heavy handed and cruel. The first reaction of a captured bird was to flutter its wings in panic and to seek a way out. It was all of little consequence now, the biggest prize he could ever hope for had flown, oblivious to his good intentions and the submission of who needed whom the most.

Before collecting the box trap and call bird from the pig shed, he replaced the inner door handle and removed the spring lest he be the victim of his own cunning, lamenting what could have been. Could it have been done differently? Given another chance what options were there? Idly he picked at the last blackberry fruits to hand before they shrivelled into nothingness. They were bitter to the taste. An hour had passed, but time had little meaning, only serving to punish his own actions with its allowance for reflection. How could it be a life so previously unexamined, would cast a void to punish the perpetrator and not the captive?

The self-flagellation was cut short when at last the faint call of a bullfinch responded to the call bird as they took in turn to reply, like talkers in human terms. Though by its secretive nature still unseen to his keen eye, the peep gradually increased in volume as it neared. He scanned the near naked hawthorn trees for a sight, and two minutes later it appeared, edging along the same hedgerow top as the box trap, waiting, calling, advancing a little at a time, and repeating the process. He could see it quite clearly now. A male beautifully pink-chested, slate grey back, a striking black cap, wing tips and a stout neck that gave rise to its name. It was stunning. So shy, more often seen than heard, despite its majestic appearance.

After some time, it worked its way along the hedgerow with nervous hesitancy until daring to perch above the box rim and espying the seeds. This was the moment. There was nothing he could do now. Either it would enter the trap or fly away. After what seemed an eternity, it dropped onto the perch which gave way, allowing the door to drop down before the bird could react. It fluttered frantically to no avail. It was trapped. A consolation prize.

CHAPTER NINE

"Enter!" Commanded the owner of the voice the nameplate on the door referred to.

John Emery was conscious of the 'clack' his new leather soled shoes made across the floorboards of the superintendent's office, and was glad to cross the room and find sanctuary on the thin, brown carpet. It supported a large desk, a stout chair for the incumbent and one other for visitors, much thinner and plastic, the furthest being occupied by Henry Adams who was returning a large, black Bakelite telephone receiver to its cradle. It had long been suspected by more regular visitors, that this was a standard habit, giving the impression of someone who was interminably busy, though the desk itself was sparsely filled, like Adams himself whose pinched shoulders and thinning, freckled scalp belied an affable, if not dithering manner. Behind him the large casement window, crisscrossed with black blast tape overlooking the courtyard, denied even more meagre daylight to permeate. It seemed that was rationed as well.

Six months into the job at the inner London reformatory school and it was only the second time Emery could recall visiting the inner sanctum of 'Caesar' as he was privately referred to by staff. Adams gestured his earnest young master to take the plastic seat with an expansive wave. His enthusiasm for the local amateur dramatic society often spilled into his daily life and was prone to princely motions and figures of speech.

"Now," Adams took up the initiative, holding up ringless hands in mock defence against the expected haranguing. "Before you say anything, I need to explain a few things, see. All my fault as such, I should have taken you into my confidence earlier, but there were things going on behind the curtains, so to speak, and then there was the matter of being privy, see?" Emery clearly didn't. Both men adjusted their posture in the acceptance this was going to take a few minutes.

"So, here's the nub, old chap. I was on the bench see, when the case came up. Tricky one, not unique of course, but unsavoury no less for all that. Errant father, mother hospitalised with consumption, taken in by an uncle, you know the sort of thing." A rolling hand waved in the air as shorthand for an all too familiar tale.

"Alleged mistreatment and abuse began to rear its ugly head —"

"I'm sorry sir" Emery interrupted "I wasn't aware of anything so dreadful but the disruptive —" Keen to air his grievance he was already feeling the wind taken from his sails.

"That is," Adams raised the stop sign again. "Abused in the way a man shouldn't abuse a boy, see?" Silence prevailed long enough for mutual understanding. "It goes on and on, until one day the boy turns on the uncle with a knife. Uncle swears he's lucky to be alive, insists on pressing charges." Adams dropped his voice as if in confidence. "Met him at the hearing you know, Rum sort. Not a very appealing fellow. The thing is —" He leant forward some more conspiratorially "The thing is, Marjorie — Mrs Buckley that is, took against uncle soonest and chaired a motion to put the boy under our guardianship until the final reports are made. Too young for some of the extreme alternatives so my hands were tied, see?" He sat back satisfied his position had been made clear.

John Emery began to see very clearly. Not for the explanation, tragic though it was, but for the position the principal had allowed himself to be boxed into with his admiration for the said Mrs Buckley a well-known weakness.

As a governor of the school, her occasional visits reduced Adams to a fawning serf in his eagerness to please. It was suspected the amply bosomed lady was fully aware of his smitten ness, and took full advantage.

Still feeling he had a point to make and justify his request for a meeting, Emery pressed on.

"Now that I am in possession of the fact's sir, I can see the boy has had a dreadful start. It's just that he's been such an unsettling influence, constantly fighting and being disruptive —" Adams held up a palm again as if stopping traffic, which essentially, he was. A bumper-to-bumper list of grievances, he allowed himself a smirk.

"Fear not dear fellow, for I have the balm to heal your wounds" He announced grandly. "The reason I am able to take you into my confidence is that it is all solved, see? You have pre-empted a meeting of staff I shall call this afternoon, but I know I can rely on your discretion in the meantime." He sat back and joined his hands over his stomach in the manner of a man who had just enjoyed a large meal.

"This morning I have been in conversation with the borough council and the board of governors. Our esteemed establishment has been given notice to evacuate our young charges to safer pastures, details to follow. So, as you see, a ready-made solution has come to our rescue, and all our little seedlings will be scattered far and wide to grow and flourish as they may, away from under the dark cloud that looms. Of course, our own immediate futures will be affected…"

Henry had had a little time to consider his own,

a large part of which included a self-invited stay with his widowed sister, who had a cottage in Scotland where he could indulge in some much-neglected fishing.

"I see, sir" John Emery was taken aback at the news and blurted his response without irony. "But I mean — how will that affect the boy; will he be part of this evacuation? I'm beginning to see how it could be a benefit to him, different surroundings could —" again, Adams help up a palm. As far as he was concerned, all the little boxes had been ticked and he was in no mood for negative derailments. The bonny banks of Scotland were beckoning.

"Ah the little thorn in your paw, you mean. No, no, of course not. He will need supervision. Marjorie will understand I did my part and I assume he will be returned to the relevant authorities to be dealt with. So, there it is, see? All tidy with bows on" He smiled in satisfaction. The young master's grievances had taken a U-turn and, now he looked at the troubled boy in a fresh light, perhaps he had been too quick to judge. He could see this constant passing on of the hot potato was of no benefit to him.

"Really Sir? Perhaps in the best interests of the boy this might be an opportunity to break the cycle of authoritative —"

"Out of my hands" Adams had allowed enough time on the matter. "Now I must telephone the good lady and liaise, so much to do" The audience with the idealistic young man was over and he lifted the receiver to underline so. Emery rose, moodily contemplating the different tone his thoughts had taken in these last few minutes.

"And Emery" The headmaster called to his back, "I shall be looking for volunteers, coordinators to help with the exodus. I trust I can rely on your input?" Emery nodded, still in thought turned to his superior quizzically. The shoes went quiet.   "The boys name, Thorn?"

"Sharpe sir, Sharpe"

"Thorn — Sharpe — oh very good." Adams amused himself whilst dialling the familiar number.

CHAPTER TEN

He had stumbled blindly into a surreal world of hideous evils. A vast alien landscape of emptiness. A warped, back of a spoon world of continuous bending, shifting, shapes where not a straight line existed. A malleable, ever-changing contour of twists and curves that bowed and whistled, groaned and creaked. A world that openly flaunted its khaki of greens and browns, not as camouflage but as pride of its unimaginative uniform.

Here there were no solid walls of one huge building after another, no right-angle corners, iron railings, or concrete edifices that defined boundaries. No maze of hardened roads to guide one's way, being trampled underfoot by the milieu toing and froing. No familiar structures to identify and give re-assurance of one's bearings. No hubbub of traffic or chatter, of blaring horns and yells, of slamming doors, music, rattling and banging. There was no one here. It was people that created noise. Only the muffled sound of his own footsteps on grass.

Huge defoliating trees stood as towering barriers to an endless vista, the infinite stretching sky that brought foreboding with its heavy bruises of blacks, purples and morbid dark greys. Sometimes with clouds so burdened with rain they might fall to the ground under the weight at any moment. Here hedgerows stood as solid and impregnable as houses, with armour that bit and scratched, pricked, and stung. Thick vegetation that tormented with their enticing offers of fruit, nuts and berries that teased with the sweetness of blackberries, sloes, rowan and wild raspberry, then played its game of evil trickery with bitter, sour and poisonous offerings that brought on severe cramps and nausea. Undergrowth that harboured snakes and huge spiders, vile insects and bugs, nettles and thorns that tore at the flesh.

A place where the very earth steeped and sloped, altered its form in strides from rock hard, to spongy soft sucking mud, or tangled roots spread overground to trip and snag the unwary or have gaping holes as an alternative boobytrap. It did not want visitors and laid enough defences to drive away any foolish interloper.

At night when all around was plunged into a deep well, where not a pinprick of light prevailed, where stars were snuffed out by low cloud, the compulsory silence weighed like a heavy blanket, stabbed at random by a piercing shriek or hellish yelp that froze the body. A torture of the senses and with each new horror followed its crony, death. Death in the form of several pied corpses of magpies he had once stumbled upon, hung along a gibbet of barbed wire like condemned criminals, or in a brace of eyeless pheasants that swung from the door of a shed he had once trespassed, only to be betrayed by barking dogs in a rabid frenzy and forced to make a hurried exit. Death in the explosion of bloodied white feathers that lay like a snowy carpet around the shredded carcass of a swan in a field, ripped apart by a predator, a parody of its formerly dignified self as an alabaster vase violently smashed into a thousand shards. Even of his own near demise in cheating its fatal grip from the rhine, like life and death were one and the same.

Even with the tendency to isolate himself and raise the drawbridge of contact in the midst of company, it was a sobering discomfort to accept the physical distance between himself and the next soul. While the body craved for its own needs of food and warm shelter, his mind urged for its own nourishment and there was nothing here to sustain it. He might as well have landed on the moon.

It wasn't so much the first breaking of daylight, more a diluting of the darkness, when the first crack of gunshot rang out to echo in the stillness, closely followed by another. The first he'd ever heard, but unmistakable for all that. What bird or beast had joined the defunct this time? From a flitting nap of exhaustion, he was startled instantly and stirred to feel the protesting pains of aching bones. Like a mouse exiting its hole he crawled out from under a small wooden bridge that spanned a black water chine, raising his head and listening about inquisitively. Direction and distance of the disturbance was hard to gauge but warning enough that trouble was nearby, just as it had always seemed to be. It was time to move on, to another somewhere.

For three long days and nights he had skulked this terrain like a quarry, keeping to the edges of fields, steering around isolated habitation, ears pricked to the sound of a voice, eyes darting all about, alert to human form. As yet, there was no building a plan of action, no purpose of journeys end. Only the instinctive reaction to break the chain, take control of his own self. But now in doing so he had become little more than a bedraggled wretch, ironically in the worst state ever as far as his physical well-being, whatever strength of search had begun for his repatriation into the fold, the cost of avoidance had left him in a pitiful state.

The near drowning had resulted in a severe chill, constant shivering making every muscle ache. Leaden limbs, pained with the trudging efforts to find warmth, food and shelter. The frail body screamed for its basic needs as he pushed on, one step at a time like an automation.

It had taken all the next day to drive most of the moisture from his inadequate clothing, a favourable drying wind and his own meagre body warmth the saviours from severe illness. Hauling himself onto the bank with the aid of the grip on tall grasses, he'd lain on his back from some time, breathless and utterly exhausted, then stripped and wrung the belted coat of water as best he could. A short-sleeved jumper and knee length trousers may have aided movement under water but offered little protection now they were reduced to little more than stained and torn rags. Wet leather sandals squeaked and squelched, socks covered painful blisters that grew on both heels. Under a film of grime, his legs and arms were a myriad of lacerations and mud. White pupils bore out through a mask of encrusted dirt on his face, short brown hair stuck down to the scalp with the stickiness of dubious substances. If this self-inflicted punishment was supposed to be an attempt to take control of his own destiny, he was making a poor job of it. This hostile land was slowly sucking the fight, as if to goad and ridicule his ability to adapt. At least if the flickering temptation to concede and place himself once again into the mechanism of autocracy won the day, the physical torture would be over. But at what cost? Placing himself once again into the calloused hands of his elders and officialdom in any of its guises would only bring its own wretchedness. Suffering as he was, there was a tiny spark of liberation, his life entirely at the mercy of his own doing now. If the fates were mocking to see how he had fared by his own volition, so be it. There was no one to depend on, never had been.

Even that teacher who smuggled him aboard the train in the chaos of evacuation without any explanation and a few curt instructions, less imperious than the others, had unwittingly conjured the circumstance of the reverend. Reminded of the ogre again and all the other authoritarian faces who decided his welfare, a dogged determination drove away any idea to concede.

That, and a cynical acknowledgement his actions in escape might have for once affected him to be the cause of attention rather than indifference, bought some solace to his predicament. No, he must go on. It would get better, it had to. Warmth, food and shelter again. They hung like the three fates.

Whatever weak daylight strained it was nulled by a bank of rolling fog that chased along the terrain, swallowing up the outlines of hedgerows and trees. The perpetrator of the gunshot would indulge in no further sport, for now he was safe from being observed. Following the line of a blackberry bush that was draped in intricate lace-like cobwebs sparkling with droplets of dew, he searched for a break in the boundary or a gate, breath forming into thick, white clouds. A chance finding of a discarded plastic sack was ripped into a makeshift cape, repelling most of the clinging moisture of the air.

In the previous days there had been the odd figure going about their business, and from a safe vantage point he would observe their strangely unhurried manner, as if time had no meaning. There was no busying of industry, no urgency of purpose. In the winding lands sometimes chancing in respite from the unforgiving land, the oncoming clop of hooves or the rumble of a car engine would send him scurrying for cover, proving a purpose for the seldom used arteries. That so few people could live in such a large area and appeared to do so little, was beyond understanding.

The smoky fog broke here and there to afford a few yards of view, then quickly closed ranks again like wet, grey drapes thick enough to cut through, one such momentary exposure revealing a wooden gate ahead. Then it was gone again. Blindly he trudged on, with the watery squeak of his footsteps breaking the submissive silence. That this portal would offer anything other than more unforgiving pasture was doubtful, but, nevertheless, food, warmth and shelter, the colossus of human needs, begged for attention. With weary sinews he mounted the obstacle and sat atop it for a rare moment in confidence of his concealment and pondered. Despite the urge to drive a wedge of distance between himself and human habitation, the latter was the only thing to save him.

Descending the gate was like immersing into steamy water, once again the fog all enveloping, his sandals feeling hard churned up ground beneath, sunken small holes from the feet of cattle, rocky ground here, soft cloying mud there, ankle deep. Progress a few more feet, it might improve. Then he stopped.

From what seemed like the bowels of the earth came a low thunderous groan that shook his body and filled his ears. A deep painful wail that rose in pitch like it was dragging itself up in suffering. It might have been the voice of fog itself. Fear tingled his spine and froze the skin. The reverberation rang through his muggy head, he stumbled backward and fell to the ground. The fog swirled and eddied all around, before a huge headed beast bore down, demanding to learn his presence. Snorting expelled air through huge flaring nostrils, it stared down with boring eyes as big as cricket balls. The great hulk of its huge body was swallowed back into the fog, as it unleashed another sonorous blast that trembled the very air.

A cow. It was a cow! An innocuous dumb cow that had put him on his backside and terrified the wits out of his already drained reserves. He scrambled to his feet in a rage of humiliation, the beast retreated into the ingesting wet shroud. How much more of this had he to endure? Nothing but hardship lay behind ever since his arrival, and god only knows what was waiting in the wings.

Once more the billowing fog broke a pocket of visibility enough to expose the sight of a small, brown, doe-eyed calf with four white socks. It stood temporarily astray from its mother and bayed in high pitched imitation of the bellow that had left him mortified with shame. Was it too making its own attempt to join in the mocking of a stranger to this land? At one with the clawing fingers of branches, pitfalls of black water, the wily trickery of forbidden fruit? Even the blackbird that would explode from a nearby hedge with an alarm shrill enough to startle the unsuspecting intruder.

In a blind fury, he ran at the stray animal with arms outstretched and shoved it vengefully with a grunt of effort. Unprepared for the attack, the calf toppled over with ease. An unexpected splash of water. He was confused. The fog parted once more, revealing a pitiful sight. A stone trough had lain behind the animal and now it lay helplessly on his back, wedged tightly, four white socks waving in the air in desperation. It began to emit a choking, gurgling scream as water gushed into its lungs, drowning the horrific noise. The boy froze at the pitiful sight. The victims terrified white eyes looking fit to burst from their sockets under the surface, spindly legs flailed uselessly in a vain attempt to manoeuvre. It was stuck fast in a watery coffin. The fraught mother appeared from the fog and began to bellow pitifully over her new-born, her distressing howl filling the air once more.

He put his hands over his ears to shut out the pandemonium, still unable to find movement in his petrified legs. The calf bent its head up as best it could but couldn't break the surface and gurgled and bleated, choked and mewed. The cow hit new notes of utter anguish, one or two of the herd shuffled into the picture in curiosity. As he stared at the appalling scene, the fog closed in again and swallowed the sight like the tableaux in the last act of a play. Only four white socks could be glimpsed before the curtain came down.

He managed to find movement in one backward step, then another, turned and stumbled blindly into the all-enveloping fog. Once again death would have the final say, as it did for all things.

CHAPTER ELEVEN

The very earth that had weaned and sustained him, made him grow, the source of all that he became, pulled Clem irrevocably downwards as if it had decided to reclaim its progeny, earth to earth, dust to dust. With every battling stride he sank deeper into the wet, black mire. It pulled at his boots, yanked at his pained legs and clung to the hem of his sodden raincoat, drawing him deeper into its embrace. It became a foe wanting to devour him, a mother earth offering comfort to her bosom one final time. It giveth and it taketh away. His weakened knees fought to resist.

His bony, gnarled hands held a death grip on the wildly bucking wooden handles, like a lifeline thrown to a drowning man. Not for dear life, an anomaly in itself, but a stubbornness to endure all the agony and suffering as was his due punishment for all his wretched failures. Self-loathing was the cloak that bore him down these past years, shame and guilt the heavy stones that filled his pockets. Its tonnage bent his back, sunk his shoulders and broke his soul under the burden. Self-pity had manifested into self-punishment for all he had done, and more often failed to do, that brought the farm to its death-knell. He fought on through the morass, not for redemption even, it was too late for that.

The old pony, kicked from its slumber and bewildered at the midnight hour, stiff from lack of exercise and sore from the ill-fitting harness, struggled to pull the blades through the cloying mud. It shied to avoid a sharp kick across its flanks and cowed at the murderous curses from its rear. It tottered and reeled, tripped and staggered, fought and battled slowly on, as did its master, only one of them by choice.

Earlier in his bed, the demons had come again to have their fun, to mock. Haze from the assuaging cider jug had thickened and formed into blackening cloud, all at once stifling and stultifying. The familiar transition to earlier times began to unroll its visions like a well-worn newsreel. But there was nothing new to be seen. The tense build up to its climax would always be the same.

"No!" He hollered "No more!" Scrambling from his bed like it was suddenly infested he leant against the cold plaster wall, panting for breath. Running long nailed fingers through his thin, damp hair, he starred at the bed like an accuser, as though the berth itself was the keeper of his secrets and crimes. It was then he finally ceded. To banish the devils, he would bow to their wishes and join them if it were to give him final peace. It was to be on this earth or under it.

A bitter easterly wind brought needles of rain that stung the flesh and blinded with its intensity. Rolling black clouds scudded across an irregularly casting moon, at times picking out the tops of trees and hedgerows as their only navigation. Every sinew tore at Clem's debilitating frame, every wracked breath rattled in his chest. Already an hour had passed into his self-imposed scalding, and only a ditch wide strip in the earth was the mark of their labour. Time and again, one mud clogged boot sank into the quagmire of spongy soil one after the other, sometimes getting stuck fast and having to use the momentum of the pulling pony to free himself.

Will and Alby leant over his shoulder, his parents too, who had reared their brood from these very

fields, his forefathers even, who had laid the foundations
for the Bottles to eek out a living from the earth. They all
swam around in the periphery of his conscience, shaking
their heads in denunciation of his actions, tutting at his
failure.

And then there was Grace. Oh Gracie! The worst
sin of all. The devoted little sister who followed them
everywhere, who gave her love and trust to her brothers
without reservation. The spirited young woman who had
taken on her mother's role with gusto, lala-ing through
her days.

That night. The awful night the news came. The
boys were lost, never to return. The hollow sickness as
he walked into their shared bedroom, single beds side by
side, boots at the foot never to be filled again. Alby's
collection of birds eggs in a sawdust tray laying on top a
chest of drawers. Will's precious books lined up on the
windowsill. The swivel wooden framed mirror on the
washstand that would never reflect their faces again. He
had collapsed onto the bed sobbing, sitting head in
hands, howling in pain. She heard, even then stronger
than him, and came to comfort with young arms around
him in mutual grief, rocking him like an infant. The
sweetness of her lavender water filled the air like a balm.
He nested a tear-soaked face against her neck, choking
in sorrow, then flush with the injustice, a farrago of
passions churning in his broken heart. Then he found
himself on top of her.

Did they know, these ghosts? Did they somehow
contrive him to suffer for all his days as a penance? If so,
he would accept it willingly, and more. Whatever it took
for their forgiveness he would endure gladly, for there
was no more severe judge, nor worse punishment, than
that to which he had sentenced himself. There was no
righting of his wrongs, even with this tardy attempt at
redemption for the death of the farm by his own hand,
they were etched too deep like physical scars, always
there as a reminder, like the boy. Who, even now, he

could barely acknowledge, who was the everyday taunting of his wrongs. The boy he spurned as the manifestations of his sins.

Through the compressed darkness the deep boom of a bittern called like the slow toll of a funeral bell, above the noise of the rain slapping his waxened coat and the sucking of mud at their feet. Cold rivulets ran off his exposed head and down his neck to mingle with the hot sweat of his toil until the two became one.

The pony, still confused as to its expectations and the unearthly hour, exhausted by the severity of its task, would lose momentum at intervals and stop, only to be driven on again under the sting of a biting whip. Clem slipped and tottered, sank to one knee and recovered in time to avoid being dragged along, or worse as he saw it, being left behind and failing once again. He would endure all of this if it took his last breath and if his end for which he had been in preparation for some years should come to fruition, so be it.

Rolo took the bolt gun in hand and stepped down from his wagon, his countenance changed into a rare sombre mood. The morning had begun fresh and damp, with a bright sun and keen breeze drying out the dripping hedgerows from overnight rain like crisp laundry. Puddles, big and small, glistened silvery against the brown earth. He had needed a basket of peat blocks for his charabanc stove and his instincts proposed good timing which would be rewarded with breakfast at Misserly. Instead, he found mayhem.

Jem had run up from the lower field, devoid of his usual enthusiasm and with a grave look never before seen, gesturing frantically for Rolo to return with him. The scene he came upon was abhorrent. Clem lay face down in the mud, unmoving, his clothes saturated. A distance away the pony lay on its flank, dirt caked and able only to raise its head at their arrival, snorting and wide-eyed in distress, as it had done for some hours. Still harnessed to the overturned plough shares, its foreleg lay out at an obscene angle. Broken straps stretched behind the twisted plough in newly cut crooked furrows. It told its own story. With a mighty heave, Rolo scooped the old man onto his broad back and wrapped the thin arms over his shoulders and around his neck. The load felt like an empty cadaver, though he could feel a wheezing, shallow breathing in his ear. He marched across the mire and back across the yard where Grace joined him in a terrible fluster, circling and begging for answers where there were none.

Having settled Clem into the house for her care, the immediate task of returning to the pitiful sight of the animal with the gun made him momentarily riled. The old beast was never in a condition for this. Retired from all but the lightest work it was seeing its last days out in dull leisure. Clem should have known better, did know better. What was he trying to do? The furrows were evident enough, but in last night's conditions with this ageing animal?

He bent to stroke a comforting large hand over the white blaze of the wet matted forehead and rested the barrel behind its white, terrified eyes.

"Alright son, all over now" he murmured. He stood with a resignation to fetch the doctor for Clem and his winch cart for the pony, his belly still rumbling for the now never to be had breakfast.

Where had Jem got to? He tried to recall the last time he'd set eyes on him, following on behind with the rescue of Clem, he assumed. Had this rotten state of affairs affected him to find his own company elsewhere? It certainly wasn't like Jem not to be at Rolo's assistance, however onerous the task. But then of late, Jem had been less than himself, somewhat distant, as if his mind were somewhere else entirely.

'Fool.' The four large letters were scribed in large capitals. The word swam before his eyes like motes, brandished on his lenses. Even with his rudimentary grasp of literacy there was no doubting it. Returning to the discovery with heart pounding, he was half afraid it wouldn't be there, whatever its dismissive tone. He had slunk away from the commotion to ruminate over what he'd found. An attempt at communication? A taunting, like in a game? The dead pony, half dead Clem, they were all secondary to the churning of his thoughts that were stirred over and again.

Earlier, the feeding of the cattle was broken by mother's frantic alert of the missing old man and on her insistence, he earnestly scoured through the outbuildings, suddenly recollecting Rolo's tragic tale of the suicidal neighbour. Once all haunts had been exhausted, he'd thrown open the pig shed door more as a gesture of diligence than likelihood. It was there he found it, deeply etched in the old tables surface with what must have been something like a large stone. The wire bird frame had been pushed to one side to make room for the foot high message. 'Fool.' Time stood still; his heart pounded. Brown pupils enlarged, fixated on the etching, trying to make some sense of it, until his preoccupation was snapped from the enigma by his mother's urgent pleas once more. On rubbery legs he dragged himself away from the discovery, only to be baffled by the sight of an empty pony stall. What on earth could it mean? Were they linked? It was only a wider search in the morning light that revealed the chaos of lower field. And now that the tragedy had unfolded and he found himself surplus to the needs of the casualties, the new obsession once again took over.

Ridiculously he was apprehensive to pull open the door again, even only having done so a few minutes before. Afraid the phantom was there, terrified he was not. It could only mean one thing. He had come back! Or even never left or returning only to leave his provocative message. But he had been here and that was all that mattered. As a gibe, it failed. Jem had long since recognised his own folly in assuming he could trap and possess the boy like one of his Bullfinches and took no offence at the message. With trepidation he entered the shed strangely feeling like an intruder in crossing the threshold, having surrendered his own domain. Hungry eyes scanned each dark corner, half afraid of another attack. Nothing moved, save the old call bird hopping from perch to perch in its cage hung high on the far wall. His muddle of traps, rods and such restored after the chaos of his first encounter, remained neatly in place. Little evidence that anyone other than himself had been here at all. Only that word. It almost become a prize possession in itself. Tangible evidence. He wondered to it again, and stared, traced a grubby finger along the scarring letters then stopped, dumbfounded. The last letter. It wasn't an 'I.' Whatever tool had been utilised to carve the word had slipped and a feint, but definite curve was visible. A 'd.' Food! The boy was demanding food! Oh, the dizziness of confusion! Joy of joys! The rictus grin broke over his face, all previous torments of the morning forgotten in an instant. That he alone was being relied upon to hold the secret, to supply the needs of the refugee was enough.   Again, a broiling of urges and ideas tripped over each other for dominance. He would lay proof of his good intentions with the furnishing of whatever were the boy's needs, for certain. If only he would come out of hiding and place himself in Jem's newfound protective shield. He almost wanted to call out for the boy. Already he felt a loyalty to the obligation placed at his feet, feeling taller in his boots in an instant. The more he could provide, the more he was depended upon. The more the gratitude owed to him would result in a loyal friendship with endless possibilities. Bang! The door slammed shut, plunging everything into the gloom. Frantically he turned to push it open again which it did with ease. A gust of wind. There was almost an inevitable sense of change. The wind of change.

CHAPTER TWELVE

Rolo was holding his small, but devoted audience enraptured, as he came to the conclusion of another of his beguiling tales.

"…then the bank manager looks up at un' an' says Mr Riddle, you gotter stop writin' these cheques, you got no money in yer account. Well, ol' Jimmy looks a bit baffled loike an' scratches 'is 'ead then says, well, that can't be roight oi still got six cheques left in me book!" The company at the small table erupted raucously between splutters of their drink, bringing the game of cribbage to a temporary hiatus until all had recovered their composure. All except one that was, Pop Wilkins an ancient, retired labourer who never got the joke. Leaning back on his stool, Rolo savoured another swig from an old china pot with a handle either side and a fading pheasant scene. His companions, farmer George farrow, and Pops younger brother Billy whose own grand age belied a strength that surprised many an unsuspecting arm wrestler, were gathered at the Feathers, or Gilbert's as it was commonly known, over quarts of dry farmhouse 'scrump' Red faces and blurred eyes would intensely discuss the burning issues of the day, including war strategies, the price of grass and Claudette Colbert.

No more than the size of a parlour room which indeed it still was, the solitary inn attracted a spattering of time wealthy locals on the infrequent days it opened, according to the whims of Gilbert's crusty moods. Heavily jowled with morose hang dog eyes, the man himself leant on the bar, ready to bring jollities to an end, albeit he had only opened his doors two hours earlier. The bar itself had been allowed to age with little regard to decor. Dull cream walls turned a brown tinge with time, the nicotine-stained ceiling held a single opaque lampshade with a flickering bulb. A stuffed Tench in a glass case was mounted on one wall, a poorly mounted Stoat with one eye similarly encased on a never used piano against another. Gilbert's quarters lay behind the door at his rear, containing his hectoring spouse Peggy, an ill-natured woman who rarely strayed into the bar, and on the odd occasion she did, looked daggers at everyone as though they should be better occupied with their time. That it was their sole source of income held no regard for her distaste for the imbibers, and it was no surprise whenever a bang on the floor above them warned Gilbert to take control of any merriment taking place.

"Oh-ohh" George Farrow was familiar with the protest. Any time now Gilbert would be gathering tankards for 'time' just when he felt barely quenched and attempted a distraction to the landlord.

"Ere, Gilbert, I ear'd you got yourself one o' they 'vacuees, is that a fact?" He gestured another fill from the barrel. "Waas'er like?" The landlord dully turned his back to draw from the keg and the brothers, sensing an opportunity, rose to put their own jugs on the bar.

"Missus got one, not me" he nodded upstairs to indicate his wife's latest demand.   "A girl, not too bad. Talks funny when 'er talks at all. 'Helps the missus round the house." The drinks were poured, and the patrons felt safe to relax a little longer.

"Oh, she got a skivvy then?" Dared Billy.
Gilbert frowned.

"What another one?" Piped up George unable to resist the barb. It would be the last pint they would drink that day. Rolo didn't mind. His own consumption had been tempered by a cracked rib incurred two days previously at Grasston horse fair.

After the debacle of Clem's idiocy, he had fermented on the welfare of Grace and Jem. With the loss of the pony the farm was brought to the brink, and it was no fault of theirs the precious Peat income would suffer as a result. Aged as the animal was, it was still strong enough to pull the cart and for their sakes he felt obliged to repair the damage. The pair had long since held a particular place in his affections for his own reasons, and he resolved to help.

Squatting on his haunches before a neatly arranged campfire over which hung a huge black samovar in preparation for nettle tea, he was pleased to abut with the patriarch of the travelling community, a thin and elderly character who nonetheless crouched with ease likewise, to attend the flames. His dark leathery skin, cracked as parchment, was as lived in as the battered old back suit he wore, now gathering speckles of ash that floated up from the stirred fire. While the camp busied itself with the erection of stalls and stages, tents and rides, Rolo opened the preamble with the chief, through whom all transactions of stock were ratified, fully aware of the protracted parlaying that tradition demanded.

The annual horse fair had toured through the county for generations, expanding over time to include an array of minor attractions to help persuade locals to part with their money. The latest inducements included the Mouse Woman, a scantily clad young temptress who sat serenely in a large cage whilst a hundred or more white mice ran amok about her, a freakshow that exhibited the foetus of Siamese twins in a large preserve jar, a stuffed two headed sheep and a dwarf dressed in an imitative pixie costume. Only the pungent smell of mouse urine, the china doll looks of the twin's heads and the off-hand manner of the dwarf tainted the experience of exotica to willing customers.

Young boys careered around the boundaries of the field at breakneck speeds on traps to show the worth of their horsemanship with trotting ponies, whilst potential buyers who gathered at the string bound sales ring bemoaned the lack of good size work beasts. Apparently most worthwhile animals had been bought by the army for the war effort which did nothing to appease them.

Exmoors, Welsh and Connemaras of little determined value by the forces were paraded, scrutinised, slapped and prodded over excitable bidding, unintelligible yelling, spitting of palms and clapping of hands.

"Now Joseph, I know 'ee to be a fair man, an' we done some good business over the years, so I'll thank 'ee for a good deal on the beast." He proffered a freshly rolled cigarette across the fire. To the surprise of the Gypsy, Rolo's interest had lain outside the parade ring in a large flat eared dun coloured mule that hung its head morosely, tethered to a horsebox near a large tent that was confirmed to be the property of King Kamil, a Latvian and resident pugilist who, for a half Crown entry fee offered a ten-shilling prize for selected challengers to last three rounds. Invited to return later while Joseph negotiated on his behalf, it was now time for a decision. In taking up their positions by the fire again, the elder lowered his voice and spoke conspiratorially, confessing a willingness to be rid of the animal from the camp.

"Tween us, he's got a queer fondness for it, y'know?" Joseph attempted to explain in his speedy brogue. "Treats it like a wife if ye gets me. Fishy lot they foreigners." Rolo's puzzled look prompted the man to embellish a further explanation, holding his forefinger and thumb together on one hand and inserting the forefinger of the other through the circle.

"Y-you mean —" Rolo exchanged his expression for one of astonishment. Joseph nodded a glum confirmation.

"Caught un at it once. Don' need the trouble, tol 'im to pack it in, but 'ee don' take no notice. Bin nowt but a pest since 'ee joined up" The old man lamented his woes as Rolo looked over at the beast in a new light, recovering from the revelation.

"Can't see the attraction meself" he managed. On hearing the boxer's terms, a purchase price of ten guineas, he winced audibly, demanding it was a mule, not a racehorse.

"One more ting," Joseph held up a hand to finish his message. "Says you gotta fight un, in the ring like y'know? Winner takes all. Itchin' for a scrap 'ee is. Now I'll tell ee sommat Roland, taint a good idea. Nuthin bedder for me t'see the bugger gone, but Kammy, well; a nasty sort y'know?" Joseph rose to his feet and rested a hand on Rolo's shoulder. "Leave 'ee t'think on it y'know?" He wondered off to arbitrate further and more regular business than this. Rolo stared into the flames and slowly removed a leather pouch from his waistcoat pocket, prepared another roll-up and stared into the flames.

A lazy string of generator fed light bulbs low in the tent canopy flickered through a fog of blue-grey cigarette smoke over a quickly gathering and expectant crowd, shuffling for position around the makeshift roped platform.

Despite the growing generosity of his girth, the challenger had a quiet confidence in his own ability to defend himself whenever the need arose. Rolo began to doubt the wisdom of his decision when the partisan supporters parted to make way and allow him to witness his adversary for the first time. King 'Kong' Kamil was huge, a giant of a man. As he climbed between the ropes accompanied by jeers and boos, the stage bounced under his weight. He paced the ring hungrily with hunched ursine shoulders, smacking his gloves together at knee height like a neanderthal. His massive tissue scarred forehead appeared to be slipping down over deep sunken eyes to form a permanent scowl. His enormous bulk sprouted black curly hair from what seemed to be every pore, while Rolo could only console himself with the thought that within three minutes of the first round his reckless decision would be over.

In his singlet and a pair of supplied leather gloves, the eager spectators helpfully manhandled Rolo into the ring, like a dubious groom might be propelled up the aisle, and now tutted sympathy at his fate. As referee, Joseph attempted vainly to herd Kamil into his corner, the ringmaster and the dancing bear. It did not begin well.

To rowdy cheers a handbell was rung, and Kamil lurched across the ring in search of his victim like a 'B' movie monster. His slow lumbering gait did nothing to encourage a weakness, hands dropped by his side, confusing his opponent from the start. Crack! Voices winced in sympathy when the patchwork forehead came crashing down on Rolo's own in a surprise attack. The recipient reeled back in shock; his senses stunned.

A weak berating from the referee gave no indication Kamil even understood English as he swept Joseph aside with a long forearm like a nuisance fly. Caught stupefied, Rolo suffered numerous clubbings from the swinging arms, alternately struggling to keep from range as the monster kept coming, taking the odd retaliatory punch as a minor irritation. Baying and booing from a blanket of flat caps threatened to drown the saving bell clang, their protests at Kamils tactics dissipating into the stale canopy air. It was abundantly clear the marquis of Queensbury rules never filtered to the Latvian, the bout more a one-sided brawl than a boxing match.

In the second, and somewhat unexpected round, Rolo managed to keep largely out of reach before he was caught in a crushing bear hug that threatened to squeeze the very life from him. Lungs screaming for air, his face smothered into a sweaty mass of stinking chest hair, then finally dropped onto the grey canvas floor to flounder like a fish on a bank. With every moment Rolo felt his strength draining, sinews hurt, ribs throbbed, his cracked head carried a splitting pain. More admonishment from Joseph failed to curtail the ogre's intention to mangle this man with whatever it took. The prize at stake had clearly enraged him like a jealous husband, clubbing his rival mercilessly. Rolo's own stubbornness in refusing to concede to this bad oaf did his health no good at all, but nevertheless a third-round bell tolled to the now yelling, fist shaking crowd, some of whom began to chant his name. Their encouragement was tempered with a communal wince of mutual solace, when a low punch sucked the air from the underdog. Skin glistening with sweat, his resistance was draining, the few jabs he landed having no visible effect, his arms feeling like lead weights, finding himself driven to the corner once more, he began to resign himself to the inevitable, while defending the clubbing blows as best he could, from the periphery of faulting vision, he became aware Kamil was winding back his great head in readiness for a final driving butt as a coup de gras. Instinctively, he dodged with the marginal speed he could muster, ducking his head under a great sweaty armpit before it came crashing down to finish him off. As a result, the fervent assembly exhaled as one. Kamil's powering forehead had collided with the ill-padded corner post. His legs buckling like a shot bull elephant, comatose before he collapsed in a heap on the floor. An explosion of cheers, followed by tossed caps, and minor scuffles as they fought to retrieve them again, broke among the melee, some of whom aided the embattled victor from the ropes with unwelcome backslapping and hugs.

Removed of the gloves and reacquainted with his shirt and waistcoat, he was helpfully dressed and carried aloft into the chilly night air, filled with the redolence of diesel fumes, between guy ropes and into the beer tent, where well-wishers pressed pints of cider laced with gin into his swelling hands. More than one supporter swore they had wagered on him though no winnings were proffered as evidence.   Though he demolished the offerings with gratitude he was fast succumbing to the fatigue of his exploits. It was time to go. The object of his challenge would need a three mile walk to be rested overnight at his camp in the woods before its new home and it was time to collect the bounty.

The euphoria of the hour diluted with an aching rib and weary legs as he slowly picked his way between tents and ropes, leaving behind a cacophony of organ music, hollering barkers, throbbing engines, bells and chimes. The site perimeter was where Jospeh had made his base, away from the bustle where he could do business in peace.

A single yellow lantern light shone through a single splatted window of an old green painted wooden spoke wheeled caravan complete with arched roof, though no one appeared to be present. As Rolo neared, a remarkable sight stopped him in his tracks. There, tethered to a wheel with flattened ears, its head hung seemingly in shame stood the mule, though it had taken on an entirely new semblance. It had turned pure white! A ghostly apparition of itself, a glowing wraith in the paleness of the lantern light. Slowly nearing, Rolo reached out a hand to rub its bristly rump as if to need confirmation of its tangible existence and his own mental well-being. He held the hand to his face. It was wet. The animal had been painted from head to tail in whitewash! The pitiful victim emitted a low pathetic screech as if attempting to explain itself, when Rolo was mildly startled by a hand on his shoulder.

83

"Lil basterds, jes missed 'em" Joseph inclined his head over his shoulder suggesting his attempted pursuit. "Looks like Kammy's got some friends after all." He began to count large coins from the pocket of his trousers.

"Ere take it an' go" he pressed the money into Rolo's hand. "Cost me, you 'ave. 'ee won't be fightin' fer a bit. Rents the tent off me see. Min' you, all in all, it were worf it." He began to climb the wagon steps, looked once more at the forlorn animal and shook his head. Rolo was left to stare as his prize, wondering at the worth of his travails and untied the lead rope.

"Ope your worth it girl" he led the mule who still refused to lift its head, out of the camp field and down the lane where it followed without protest. A breaking new moon did nothing to lessen the phantasmic illumination of the animal.

"Thats it, keep your 'ead down. You be makin' a good target for they Jerry bombers" he advised.

CHAPTER THIRTEEN

The days began to bite with their short hours and sharp winds. Summer visitors had long since flown to warmer climes, making way for arrows of honking geese from eastern Europe to graze in the damp winter grasses. Songbirds had ceased their summer lullabies, now only the stark yak of crows and chattering of sparrows broke the quiescence. Tall Elms, denuded of their foliage, stretched ever narrowing veins until they were mere pencil lines disappearing into dull skies, black against grey. Soon enough the herd would be bought indoors for the oncoming cold months, where labours would double for their husbandry. Hedge cutting, fence repair and ditch draining would all be ignored again this year, sugar beet was still in the ground, likely to rot. The hives of peat stacks stayed high, still to be delivered. The discovery of the calf, a brief token of new life and drowned in a freak accident it was supposed, was another crushing blow for the Bottles to suffer.

Largely oblivious to the tightening stranglehold was Clem. Diagnosed with mild pneumonia and total exhaustion he was in a heavy slumber for most of the time, a bed having been made up in the parlour for his convalescence, where a warming fire was made up for the first time in many a year. The visiting doctor surrendered his insistence on hospitalisation after the patient's weak refusal to go and Grace's uncharacteristic forthright refusal to allow him. The compromised agreement was regular medical visits and doses of his sister's spoon-fed panacea of potato and pea broth, with varying degrees of cooked potato and a regular absence of peas.

An unsolicited visit from ma French left Grace in a heavy state of agitation when the old soothsayer shook her head in defeat at Clem's chances of survival after a poring of her trembling palm.

"Well, strictly speakin' she's what we call a hinny" Rolo was explaining to the young new owner. "Alf male 'orse an 'alf female donkey you see. What's called a molly mule — a girl that is. Can't breed wi 'er o' course, odd chromosomes." He witnessed a quizzical look. "Don't worry, I'll explain that another day. I tried 'er out on the cart an' she's a good puller. She'll do you right."

Jem was absorbed by the lecture as he always was when Rolo departed his wisdom but was still curious of its origin. He queried again.

"Well let's just say I won 'er up the fair" Rolo was enigmatic "Ad to knock off a coconut." They were stood in the yard buffeted by a swirling wind that sent leaves whipping in frantic circles around their legs like hooplas, two days after the horse fair had decamped for their next venue.

"Anyways" Rolo continued "I 'ad t' get the winch to get the calf out, took some doin.' Blown up like a set o' bagpipes time I got to 'un. Must 'ave been bumped by one of the 'erd. Never known anythin' like it. Now, daft thing is, they won't go near the trough now. You'll 'ave t'take buckets up till they forget about it — in the cart — she'll 'elp you." He slapped a meaty hand on the newly scrubbed and hosed animal, who was carrying her head high, ears pricked.

Jem was being addressed as the master of the farm; the reliance now being pressed on his young but yokish shoulders. It was his burden to carry.

Rolo watched the boy becoming acquainted with his new charge, gently stroking its muzzle and talking softly, to which it responded with a heady rub to Jem's chest. He led the animal away to begin their labours. Still the boy did not seem his normal self, it must be down to the calf, he thought. He held great sympathy for the boy, growing up in the increasing mausoleum of a household with no one of his own age to share his days. Clem with his uncommunicative ways, his broken body could be mended in parts, but his spirit was dead. Grace with her own mental health issues, a shadow of the woman he once knew.

In the lee of the wind, he sat himself on an empty, overturned oil drum and performed the ritual of rolling a cigarette. The doctor was with the couple at the moment and, not normally given to reminiscence, he allowed himself a rare moment to ponder. The vivid pictures of his very first encounter with the farm came as easily as yesterday.

Almost at this very spot he had approached Clem for seasonal haymaking work as a roving labourer. Still reticent and curmudgeonly even then, the man was hardworking enough, though seemingly carrying an inner burden that left him heavy of heart and totally devoid of humour. A fair enough employer though, Rolo found himself increasingly relied upon and staying longer than expected, until his wilful spirit finally succumbed to its bid for freedom and the wondering lifestyle he yearned, returning spasmodically to lend a hand. Not before however, he fell under the spell of a light and gay Grace, as she was then, with a sparkle that burned under her initial shyness.

That first summer, how she would sally across the fields at noon. The warm breeze toying with her billowing dress, with a large pitcher of cider and buttered bread for the handful of sweating help. Her long fair locks were pinned up to lend a sweetness to her fine features, a ready smile that brought dimples to ruby rose cheeks. Favouring Rolo with her company, they would take their rest propped against a hayrick, her long brown legs stretched out, topping up his mug as an encouragement to regale his outrageous tales of travels, to which in turn she would be aghast and helpless with laughter. How he would convince her he once rescued his colleagues from disaster when the roof fell in on the local treacle mines, or that once he made and lost a fortune in marketing pigeon's milk. Long into the evening they would enjoy each other's company, returning to the farm picking the hay from each other's hair.

On his return two summers later, he was taken aback to learn an infant had entered the household, its mother a shadow of the girl she once was, a snuffed-out candle. Dulled was the lustre of her innocent eyes that no longer met with his at length, the vibrancy of her movements. In its place was a fretfulness, of coping even with the mundane, that wracked at her thinning frame. As though the very sun in her heart had been eclipsed. Clem, in turn to his sister's capricious nature, had withdrawn further into himself, sour and devoid of any acquiescence to her child.

Instead of the blossoming bud of a new generation at Misserly, the young Jem was moulded into the framework as additional stock, never feted, the ambivalence of his sire hood buried with the queries it provoked. As he grew, although placid by nature and already strong, he was never once seen to seek comfort from the elders after a heavy fall or bang to the head with fits of tears. Rather, he would sit or stand stock, still determined to control his breathing then carry on oblivious of the incident. To this end he never sought or received indue attention.

As an erratic witness to Clem's indifference and

Grace's willing but often bungling attempts at motherhood, Rolo had taken time to spend with the boy and instruct him in the ways he fancied he would his own.

Snapped from the reverie by the burning butt to his fingers, he rose and headed to the doctors departing frame, still feeling the soreness of his own bones. The fight may well have been a rash thing to do, but never being one to dwell on his actions, the sight of young Jem leading the mule was just reward. Obliged to pay a sick call, he half hoped the old man had fallen asleep again. It would certainly avoid an explanation of the mule's arrival. The cur stirred at the foot of the steps but in receiving no morsels began its habitual dragging of its flanks against the wall to temporarily ease its soreness.

The kitchen was cold. Grace was sat at the table head bowed. The fire had been allowed to go out, unattended. She jerked at his arrival, sat hands between her knees like an angler on a frosty morning. The letter in her hand suggested the cause of worriment and not the doctor's diagnosis. Rolo gently took it from her hand and began to read. She looked up at him beseechingly.

Jem froze on the spot, straining his pupils wide in disbelief. No, surely not. Even in the half morning light there seemed to be no doubting it. He scarcely dare breathe, his heart thumped against his chest. A swaying dizziness scrambling all reason of what to do. Even in the constant chill of the pig shed, his palm began to sweat. He gulped. The old Bullfinch continued its tapping in its cage. Nothing else moved. A full minute passed before he dare take another step forward. There was no doubting it was true.

In the furthest corner, amongst a pile of old sacking and oddments he recognised from various parts of the farm, bundled like the making of a mouse nest, was a face. A filthy, barely recognisable set of features, but a face, nonetheless. A sleeping face. Wrestling from his paralysis he ventured a step closer, fearfully recalling the previous encounter. But this face did not seem like it was going to spring at him, it did not look fearsome or wild. He reached a hand toward the bundle of materials, then retracted it, unsure of the best approach. He lowered to his knees to study the features further. His mouth gaped open for an utterance, but nothing came. He tried again and forced a strangled 'hello' that was barely audible. Then louder. The dirt encrusted mask remained impassive. Jem leaned in closer, sensing a thrill in being this near to his obsession. With his own eyes adjusted now to the dimness he studied the features as best the grime would allow. It was a young but emaciated face, snub-nosed with high cheekbones, eyelashes were stuck with gunk, a black lipped, downturned mouth slightly ajar. Nothing else was visible under the swathe of sacking but Jem decided he'd seen enough to swallow his fears and offer his help. A breath away, he called once more. Nothing. A wavering hand reached to shake the bundle gently, then harder. Bolder by the minute he reached out to poke at a grubby cheek, flesh to flesh. In a final desperate attempt for a response, he shook the bundle forcibly hissing a loud 'wake up.' The face dropped forward in slumber.

Jem sat back disconsolate. So finally, this was him, the focus of all his attention of late, the would-be friend of his imagination now dissipated into this sad bale of rags. And now it was all too late. Dragging his eyes from the boy who held the key to his fanciful plans, he glanced at the table on which he could now see yesterday's offerings of two roughly hewn bread slices with a dripping scape lay untouched. The boy was dead.

An empty sickness gripped his stomach. His efforts hadn't been enough, thinking back to the recent days. As had become routine by now, whatever rations he could muster would be supplied during daylight hours in an unspoken understanding between the total strangers, when the shed was vacant. As long as the food was taken, Jem dare not breech the agreement after his initial clumsy efforts and the boy took flight for good. Wherever the fugitive took himself during these times was a constant torment to Jem who surreptitiously scanned about, terrified and thrilled he might be being observed, and the boy would finally show himself.

All for nothing, it hadn't been enough. The fragile trust bestowed upon him was broken. He reached out for the crust he had bought this morning and pushed it to the boy's lips, that it might produce a magical reflex like a girl might feed a doll. Delicately with a forefinger he lowered a blackened lip and tried to coax the bread between the teeth. He was trying to feed a corpse.

The so-called saviour sank down heavily before the bundle, still hypnotised to the lamentable features. The illusion he had wallowed in was never to be, a friend lost. The restless nights in bed planning how they would spend their days, growing to be partners on the farm even, working together with ma and pa retired, just the two of them.

How Jem would be boss of course but a kindly one, firm but fair he decided, bestowing his knowledge to a willing pupil. The scenarios had even taken place as he went about his work, mentally instructing the apprentice of his obligations.

'You gotter do it like this see?' He would say patiently or 'watch what I do,' alongside other pearls of wisdom he may bestow. But it would not be all work. There were fantasies too of the times spent to fish and trap, to swim in the pond, like those other boys. Maybe even go into Shepton and meet them. No, not that. It would be just the two of them. Now it was all dashed, never going to happen.

However, this boy had been surviving, whatever had bought him here had finally taken its toll. What on earth had he been running from that was worse than living like the rats in the barn? If only he had trusted Jem sooner. He did not even know his name, this would-be friend he sat beside as easily as blood brothers, their secret over. The elders would be told, the police would take him away. He threw the bread crust across the room in frustration, inadvertently hitting the Bullfinch cage and causing the bird to noisily flutter and 'peep' in alarm.

"Nnnnhh…." A barely audible murmur emitted from the cadaver. Snapped from his stunned confusion, Jem scrambled frantically onto his hands and knees again and levelled to the face hardly daring to believe. The features never stirred. He saw an almost imperceptible rise and fall of the cloth wrappings and felt a surge of adrenaline. Alive! The boy was alive! A wash of ecstasy drove him to tap the besmeared cheeks with renewed gusto to no avail but another faint low murmur. It was enough to send Jem into an apoplexy of panic. Alive yes, but only just. He was sick, very sick.

Fate was becoming a teasing pendulum, alternately giving and taking the boy away, but now having this tangible experience of a one-sided fellowship he would seize it with all his being.

"S'alright, I'll 'elp you, I will" A whispering croak trembled from his lips. The rush of confusion stunted the new joy of reincarnation. Help how? Ailing cattle he had dealt with, testified to births and deaths, splinted legs, aided recovery from sickness with varying results, but this? The only certainty was that he was on his own. The adults would raise the alarm, call the doctor, police whoever. Even Rolo, most likely. He daren't confide in his ally, even assured he would know exactly what to do. It would be over before it began, taken away never to return. But if he could aid his recovery, what then? Almost basking in the imagined esteem in which the patient would hold him, forever grateful for his life saving actions, indebted to his rescuer. Think. Medicine. His father was under medication, that would do it. Medicine cured. Suddenly it all became much simpler. But purloining the curative right now would be difficult. His mother was in constant attendance, but he must do something. He set to work.

With the adults occupied and Rolo elsewhere, he was free to scour through the barns for his needs unobserved. A short time later he turned to the pig shed pushing a laden wheelbarrow and set about making a bed from straw bales under a horse blanket snatched from the mule, then fired up a rusting paraffin heater that flared and spat with the choking dust it had gathered. It settled to discharge a heat that defeated the cold air. Still unfinished, he raced back to the hay barn where in the echoing silence he gathered the loose grass from the floor and stuffed it into a sack to make a fine pillow. Turning to leave he stopped. From somewhere in the barn a watery trickle could be detected. Not the excess of last night's rain, nor the cold tap that fed from the standpipe in the yard, that was broken. Edging to the rear dinginess of the barn and clambering over scattered stored planking, he stood before a heavy stand of railway sleepers formed to make a platform on which stood a forty-gallon oak cask with rusting brass rings. The wooden spigot was slightly open allowing the sweet, fermented apple juice to drip steadily onto the stone floor. Over time the acids had eaten away at the concrete floor to form a gully. The tap was closed with a protesting squeak before he stood for some moments absorbing the significance of the fresh leak.

Racing back to his patient with newly formed pillow under his arm, he lent to take a large sniff under the stubby nose. Of course! He should have noticed before, but it was an odour that permeated large parts of the farm like hay or manure until one came oblivious to it. That was it! The boy wasn't perilously ill, he was dead drunk!

Overwhelmed with relief at his own diagnosis, it became apparent the recovery was going to be a much easier affair. The boy was in no danger. It would be little different to convalescing Mr Pittar the cider maker, in his times of overindulgence. Time would bring the inebriate around, then he would see for himself Jems efforts to succour and how modestly the gratitude would be accepted. Then the newly awaited but eagerly sought companionship could begin. Unravelling the swathes and gently shipping his arms underneath the torpid body he raised the noticeably underweight sufferer and proudly laid him out onto the newly formed bed, standing back for a moment to admire his efforts like a cook may lay out a crisp Christmas goose for dinner.

From a covertly espied kitchen, thankfully devoid of his mother, he carried an enamelled basin of water scooped from the copper boiler and a matchbox sized tablet of carbolic soap. Determined to do all he could before consciousness should furnish any resistance, he began wiping the face of its filth until the features were defined for the first time, like wiping steam from a mirror. Even in repose it held a troubled expression, deathly pale skin surrounded a down turned mouth with dark eyebrows that furrowed under a heavy frown of defiance.

Satisfied with his efforts, Jem covered the boy in a heavy over blanket and sat against the wall beside him, revelling in the alliance he considered made, the unprotesting chum delighted to pick up the threads of a once improbable fantasy.

The bare cinder block walls danced with pinks and purples from the flicker of the paraffin heater, a radiance like warm porridge spread through his core. At last, it had all come together, and it felt a very special moment, the pig shed a very special place.

CHAPTER FOURTEEN

The heavy walnut framed clock signified the hour with perpendicular hands as Arthur Bolsover-cox finished his final signature with a flourish and capped his fountain pen to signify the end of another working day. Once again he bemoaned his increased workload owing to the absence of his dutiful secretary Iris. Among the two hundred or so smashed and broken souls who fell victim to a devastating bombing raid which had crippled the city of Bristol two nights earlier had been her mother, which while of course he sympathised, found to be most inconvenient. This far his demands for a temp had fell on stony ground.

Still now, motes of brick and rubble dust, ash from burning timbers of hundreds of shattered homes, factories and shops, was settling on piles of blown out walls, twisted metals, ruptured gas pipes, burst water mains, cratered roads and a devastated populace like the handful of dust to dust on a coffin.

Traumatised victims wandered bewildered, bereaved and homeless. Ambulances, fire engines and rescue teams rushed through the chaos, each hour bringing a new emergency, fresh fires, falling masonry, newly discovered bodies, the result of ten thousand or so incendiary bombs and explosives dropped on the metropolis by the Luftwaffe.

Arthur considered it a miracle his own offices had escaped a similar tragedy and made a mental note to press further to his superiors to relocate to the safety of an underground shelter as other government bodies had done, and after all the safe custody of his own work was of no less importance, now the threat had become fatally real. Why, even in his own home he'd found Mrs Bolsover-cox in a state of apoplexy as the resulting tremors reduced her prized collection of Royal Crown Derby china to fragments, as it slipped piece by piece from the Welsh dresser and on to the floor.

Donning hat and coat from the stand and carrying his briefcase, he glanced around the office one final time. Invariably the last to leave, he left and negotiated a maze of corridors and out into the sombre evening. Streetlights still undamaged were dimmed by government order, scant traffic lights still working were hooded, the odd torchlight of a pedestrian pointed downward. He walked briskly the hundred or so yards to his beloved Ford Popular, which had annoyingly collected another skin of dust, defeating his efforts. He settled gratefully from an air of defeatism that hung over the sombre streets like a black portent.

A young woman had passed by, pushing a pram loaded with meagre chattels in a stupefied state, followed by a young child who likewise stared ahead into a void. Two older men walked in single file, the latter with a hand on the leader's shoulder, the former with a guiding stick. Both had bandaged eyes. The inner sanctum of his vehicle became a cocoon as he navigated a snarl of still undamaged roads in the general direction of his semi-detached in Broadmead. First though, a diversion through empty side streets toward the docks where he cruised to a halt outside a familiar pair of Louvre doors that stood unnoticed among a terrace of disused warehouses.

Though not by nature a natural imbiber, the small

intimate bar, unremarkable as it was, provided solace for his day among the clientele of his own preference. Upon entering the dimly lit room he took in the two young men at a corner table nearest the door, engaged in earnest conversation, their lipsticked faces illuminated by the glow of a table lamp. A single young blond fellow wearing a cravat on another table looked up sharply at Arthur's entry, then sank back in disappointment at the continued absence of his intended rendezvous. The shield of the shadows seemed their predilection. Nearest the bar on a stool sat a character that looked totally unsuited to the premises, as a nun in a nudist camp. He looked large and rustic with a heavy girth, jowly cheeks with sideburns and a leather trilby. Arthur recalled he had been here the previous evening, quietly sat at a corner table, obscured by the shadowy light. Now he could see the man properly, he suddenly wondered, had he seen the fellow outside his own offices recently, idly watching the building, then quickly he dismissed the notion. The young barman was acknowledged with a rare smile and was passed a shilling for a half a bitter in his soft palm with a deliberate pause.

"Keep the change Gordon" Arthur said brightly, holding eye contact.

Pressured as he felt about his work, his modest but comfortable home was not the balm he sought to ease his woes. The confidential little establishment became his sanctuary between the two. A private haven that had thankfully escaped the bombing. He took a sip of beer and gently wiped the froth from his pencil moustache. Not too late tonight, he promised himself. Besides, with the city in turmoil the chances were there would be few punters about of his own persuasion. Allow time for the strained lady wife to retire to her bedroom, still lamenting the loss of her china. The next evening boded to be the gathering of one of her intolerable bridge parties, having decided her part in the war effort should be to maintain the equilibrium of the social mores of middle England. Arthur had already been instructed not to work long into the evening as he had done so of late, as he explained. The prospect weighed him, although the bright young magistrate of the last gathering interested him.

"Evenin'" A deep utterance snatched him from the memory. He turned to see the stranger place his glass on the bar for a refill next to his. Reluctantly the greeting was acknowledged with a nod. Now he could see the fellow properly. Blue sparkling eyes, indeterminate age, certainly not young, rather powerfully built, large rough hands with chipped nails. Definitely manual. The attire of a lockkeeper or horse trader. Oh no, not his type at all. Keen not to be embroiled in conversation, Arthur moved to the opposite stool, a few more feet away.

"Bad Business" the man persisted, drawing his stool closer.

"Eh?" The nod in deference had obviously not been taken as a hint to his unwillingness to converse. He begrudged the terse reply. Clearly the man was not going to be put off by his indifference, mildly curious as he was of the newcomer's presence.

"Bristle, Jewel o' the west, ripped apart like pearls from a broken necklace" Arthur turned at the flamboyant choice of phrase.   Clearly this chap was educated and spoke in tones at odds with his appearance. He glanced around the room. The two young men sat even tighter in their clandestine conversation, one seemed upset.

Cravatted boy looked solemnly at his watch in agitation at the non-appearance of his assignation. Oh well, he thought, may as well tolerate the intrusion for a moment, even the handsome young barman had disappeared to change a barrel.

"Come up t'see my sister in parkway when I 'eard." The stranger inched closer. "Pleased t'say she were one o' the lucky ones. Try as I may to persuade 'er t'come stay wi' me, she's as stubborn as the proverbial mule. I dunno, women, eh?" He drew heavily on his roll up. Arthur coughed not so much from inhaled smoke, more in the irony of discussing the merits of womankind in this establishment.

"Makes me mad to the marrow, a mind t' join up tommorer and fight the swine, a man of principle like yourself must feel the same, I 'spect eh?"

"Reserved occupation" Arthur was satisfied at the importance of his terse reply.

"O' course, ministry I s'pect, man o' your standin," he tapped his bulbous nose knowingly. "You can always recognise a man of intellect, vital work, you chaps. The invisible army, I say."

The flattery was not lost on Arthur who had always felt his work deserved more appreciation.

"Another one?" He gestured at Arthur's glass as the barman returned.

"No — no, I really must go" he held a spurning hand on his glass. Satisfied with this man's perception of him, he began to rise from his stool only to feel the pressure of a heavy hand on his shoulder.

"Times like this yer torn between mourning the dead and celebratin' yer own good fortune, do you reckon? You'll 'ave one for the road — two large gins please young man." The barman returned to oblige.

"No — no honestly" his curiosity now sated; he had no need of further dialogue.

"Now I don' come from hereabouts," his new companion continued oblivious to the protest "but I know one thing. Men, women an' children have all been crushed underfoot, made widows an' orphans by Jerry. As the man said 'it is forbidden to kill. Therefore, all murders are punishable, lest they kill in large numbers an' to the sound of trumpets. Mebbe its time to ponder over a higher deity after all, an' why we bin saved. What can we do to serve, eh? To the king!" His sermon complete, the man solemnly raised his glass to the portrait over the bar, downed the gin and obliged Arthur to follow suit. There was no escaping the toast. Screwing his face and putting the unwanted potion to his lips, he gasped at the perfumed dryness of the Juniper. His eyes watered and with a splutter, he finished the glass.

"Take your occupation" The stranger was like a rolling tank, his assertiveness riding roughshod over his victim. "Ministry I believe you said," although Arthur was sure he hadn't. The gin was working its way into his bloodstream creating confusion.

"I can tell by your bearing you are a man of a brainy nature, defence I 'spect, no doubt work o' the highest importance." The complimentary remarks were hard to resist, the rare appreciation of his talents weakening his resolve.

"Actually, agriculture" The stern warnings of loose talk were lost on Arthur immediately, the spirit hit home as he pronounced the second word with an emphasis. Only he could make agriculture sound more vital than defence. The impressive response fed his ego.

"Oh agriculture, well that's vital enough. The masses 'ave to be fed, army can't fight on empty stomachs. You mus' be very proud to represent the farmers fillin' the breadbasket o' the country, toilin' night an' day doin' their bit to 'elp fight the effort."

For once Arthur could not hide his derision, the gin fervently in control. He uttered a snort of contempt fuelled by the alcohol and was about to air his own views on farmers of his experience, when through glazing eyes he noted the challenging expression offered to him. Another gin was pressed into his hand, one he hadn't noticed being ordered.

"Down the 'atch," came the pledge as his glass was clinked, the salutation invited to continue. Oh goodness, he thought, desperate to find an escape from the situation. Arthur always prided himself on being in charge of his own circumstance and with this fellow he felt he had boarded a runaway train. Fighting a quease in his stomach, he drained the glass no more easily that the first, pledging this first experience of this foul spirit would be his last.

"Queer old place this," the man was taking a survey around the bar, the inference confused Arthur as to his meaning. "Forgotten me manners — Percy" he held out a hand.

"Eh? Oh, Arthur — I really must be going —" he was beginning to sway on the stool. For no reason he could fathom, he then stated his surname. "Bolsover-cox." The newcomer was still distracted by the two young men at the corner table, one of who was beginning to quietly weep.

"Do they? Doesn't really surprise me, really" he offered.

"No — no — my name".

"Ah I see, yes sorry. Rowland Percy. They call me Rolo".

CHAPTER FIFTEEN

The assault, if it could be called such, came out of the blue. For some time, the boy had lain in semi cognisance, eyes fluttering open and staring into a void, then closing again. His ramblings were half delusional, none of it making any sense to his engrossed attendant. Jem was content to keep his vigil for as long as it took. At last, he was here, the prize he cherished. With nearness and his own care, all traces of fear had dissipated. It was just a boy. Not a wailing banshee. A boy who looked at the end, needing a helping hand.

Jem's studious poring of the features couldn't reveal character, even though a fixed scowl suggested a hint of defiance. With Jem able to scrutinise the waif at his will, he wallowed in a sense almost of possession, of ownership even, like a stag beetle he once kept in a matchbox, until it escaped. He wanted to poke and pore over his find, see what it did, how it spoke, all its workings.

He was coming around, no doubt about it. Fleetingly rueing his decision not to manacle the boy and cause further distress, he could only hope the patient's condition would be enough to shackle him until a bond of trust could be built.

Under a deep furrowed brow, the dark lashes

once again began to blink open, this time for longer, until the stare came to focus first on the light from the heater, then around until he turned his head to settle on Jem sat beside him.

Without warning the dormant volcano erupted. He sprang with surprising agility at an unprepared Jem not withstanding an inferior build and weakened state. An amalgam of cold foul breath and bitter spittle flecked Jem's face which was under attack from over long fingernails, clawing and scratching, drawing a lesion that just missed an eye. Blackened teeth tried to purchase on any visible flesh, snapping and growling. Jem had had enough. Slighted that this wretch should decide to attack after all he had done, triggered a latent anger so rarely surfaced. With a long sweep of his forearm, he dismissed the attacker like an exuberant dog at play. The boy fell back onto his bed of straw, spent. Both breathed heavily, staring in mutual contempt. Jem was indignant to be treated like an enemy after all he'd done thus far to help and protect this ungrateful wretch, was this the reward he'd coveted so much? The moment he'd anticipated for so long turned into a bitter insult.

As quickly as the maelstrom of temper had risen, Jem calmed to his normal state of equilibrium. What was this pathetic heap doing to him? Bringing rise to all these sentiments never before experienced, did not know what to do with, confused at these anomalous senses. The boy had opened a box of feelings alien to his senses, and he did not know what he was supposed to do with them. Outstared, the boy dropped his defiant scowl and began to look around, taking in the bedding he was sprawled upon and the paraffin heater spreading its purplish blush on the milieu, still panting from his efforts.

"Who you told?" The croaky whisper almost inaudible even to his own ears, the first words he had spoken aloud for some time. Finally, he had uttered directly to Jem, they had contact. At first the squeaky accent, and incoherent voice surprised him. Here they were, face to face, in touch. Affronted by the accusation he retorted.

"I ain't told no one, cross me 'eart and' 'ope t' die." He genuflected with a finger across his chest, calmed by the mild thrill of conversing at last. Of all the things he'd planned to say, they would talk about, it all evaporated, an instant bond in his ideal, the gratitude, the subservience of the younger who seemed to challenge at every juncture. It was easier to allow the silence to dominate, to allow their proximity to cement itself. Which it did, until the boy abruptly leaned forward and began to dry heave. In an instant Jam scooped up the basin and held it under his chin to catch the vomit that gushed from his mouth. Another heave, a hand clutched Jem's wrist to keep him from moving, another load. The boy spat and dribbled, nodded he was done, watery eyed with the effort. With a corner of the blanket, Jem gently wiped the small chin clean of the bile and placed the basin on the floor.

"Jem, I'm Jem" he encouraged, emboldened by the hand that had reached out. The boy nodded. The information wasn't new.

"Heard your mam call you enough." Again, the way tones that pronounced its words so strangely. It was an effort for the boy to speak at all, and when he did there still seemed to be an underlying belligerence, an obduracy not to concede whatever battles he was fighting. So the boy had been lurking about the farm after all, holing up in the barns, watching Jem go about his business, the disclosure not lost on him, a mild thrill that he hadn't strayed after the debacle of his unintended capture.

In trying to contain all these thoughts Jem stood and walked over to the empty goldfinch cage, running an idle finger along the bars.

"You let the birds out?" Was all he could think of to say, regretting it might sound an indictment. A nod.

"Jus' wanted to watch 'em fly" Jem shrugged

indifferently at the semi apology. Still he hadn't offered a name, but that could wait. He was here, tangible and in order not to make the quarry take flight again, he must tread carefully. They were circling each other warily, like duelling swordsmen, albeit one in no condition to fight, but his defences apparent.

"That was your pa, out in the field?" The question took Jem by surprise. He had seen him but never helped, raised an alarm? For a fleeting second the prickle of anger rose again and subsided. Of course, there was little he could do given his circumstances. How easily he made allowances, not wanting to raise any confrontation, determined to forge this bond. Befuddled with this broiling soup of sentiments, this boy was having a perplexing effect. Only now it occurred to him how little thought he had given to his father's well-being of late, obsessed as he'd been by this sorry looking bundle. The moment he yearned for was here and unpractised as he was in the company of his peers, he felt suddenly stifled and overawed by the experience.

"I brung you some clothes" again an awkward utterance to his efforts, to outgrown trousers and a coat of his own at the foot of the bed. Another nod of appeasement.

"Oi'll get summore to eat." The need to be away even momentarily to understand whatever was churning inside him was paramount. It had begun.

Out in the yard, the pallid morning sun broke from grey, white clouds with a brightness to dazzle his eyes. He strode across, not avoiding the puddles, even possibly able to walk on their surface. The grin so unevenly streaked across his face was wider than ever. Things would never be the same again.

"Terry" the boy had said quietly as Jem closed the pig shed door behind him.

Early morning mist huge like a thin blouse around its base, the Tor exposed like a provocative firm breast over the wetlands, St Michaels tower its ripe nipple. The ancient Isle of Avalon where legend insisted Joseph of Arimathea chose to plant the holy thorn, looked nobly over the somnolence of the surrounding levels. Its lush pastures were now beginning to fill with the seeping flood waters as it always had at this time. Cattle were soon to be husbanded indoors to be indulged in the more costly silage and barley, cold easterly winds shivered the settling waters into hardened ripples that chased each other across the silvery surface.   Curlew and lapwing had moved in, probing in the soft earth for insects and larvae. Majestic standing heron, still carrying the cold stare of their prehistoric ancestors patrolled the rhines, statuesque in the patient search for frogs and eels. The bones of trees stood dead seemingly, never to recover, clouds hung heavily as if to defy gravity. The land was going into its annual petrification where neither seed nor harvest, growth nor procreation would trouble it for these cold months.

Some days had passed and after exhaustive enquiries through the hamlets and scant searches thereabouts, the hunt for the absconder had been handed over to the county constabulary. It had been concluded he had made his way to one of the larger populaces of Taunton or even further and was lying low. Along an otherwise empty lane, the newly settled mule rhythmically clopped, causing numerous rooks and crows in adjoining fields to rise protestingly in the air, circling and screaming their harsh outcries.

Jem had loaded the peat cart the previous evening and had gained a large coup in persuading a reluctant Terry to accompany him on the errand with an enigmatic confidence in the absence of danger of exposure. As a compromise a tarpaulin covered the wagon which the hideaway would steal under in an instant should the need arise. Still, he was dubious of Jems surety of his safety, the confident boy unwilling to explain further. Flicking at the reins with a beaming smile was Jem, with a nervous looking companion at his side. At intervals, the elder would stare at the passenger and spread the crooked expression as though he held the secret of joy.

The boys had settled into a haphazard routine of Jem's provisions and the newcomer's recovery. Terry had gradually regained his strength and a wary confidence in his refuge for the time being. Averse as he was to relinquish control of his own immediate fate, previous experience proved his inadequacies in surviving in those surroundings alone. For now, he would accept the basic shelter, though often finding Jem's exuberance irritating, he lost himself among the barns during the day for respite. Constant questioning of his motives, the assumption of his long-term future at the farm all became the price he paid for the mild comforts.

For now, he sank his woollen capped head inside the collar of an oversized borrowed coat, along with the other articles of Jem's. For all his doubts of the wisdom of this jaunt, it was at least a chance to escape the confines of the pig shed that was almost becoming a punishment in itself. Even being able to view over the tops of hedgerows he had once prowled, even the emptiness that stretched to the blue distant hills beyond at one time so punishing, began to offer a sense of freedom from the visual claustrophobia of late. Occasionally he would cast furtive glances about, reassured by the vast void once so daunting. The need for concealment was abating, as was the foreboding of treachery that had almost become second nature. But it was his suspicious nature that had become his first line of defence and he was loathed to relinquish it. Heaving, he placed his paper-thin trust in this queer fish, albeit someone who had supplied his needs without any demands for recompense, save the company he craved.

It became apparent to Terry the solitude and plainness of the farm and its surroundings was deep rooted into the soil and the boy was a product of it.

There was an open honesty, a simplicity in Jem he saw as his own potential undoing and he was allowing himself to be cajoled into a venture such as this, at odds with the sceptical barrier he had built.

"Be alright, oi promise, you'll see" he'd said. Jem had taken control of the reigns, literally, and the inner fight in Terry plunged him deep into contemplation of his own intent, to break away from the farm and the dependence that was a consequence of it. As yet he'd made no plans and had only survived one day at a time, but now with restored strength had ample opportunity to mull over his mistakes. There was no regretting to flee from the melee at the station and the odious preacher, but to be plunged into this backwater of nothingness had exacerbated his misery. Looking across the horizon now, it seemed impossible that a city could be somewhere not too distant, that this rough green table ran on forever. That a big town even, a thriving urban sprawl familiar to his nature was out there, where he knew the language of the streets, where bustling crowds were oblivious to each other, absorbed in their own business. Where he would walk openly, where abundant opportunities offered themselves in busy shops and markets., all that was second nature. Action, noise and a fusion of smells would swallow him greedily, whereas this foreign territory spat him out. But first to prioritise, find out exactly where this was and to prepare properly. Running blindly had taken its toll. If he were to survive by his own means there must be a fitting strategy for his exit, never again to sink this low. Here he was, jostling along in a mule cart in the middle of nowhere, ready to dive onto a pile of stinking peat at any moment, in the hands of this simpleton who clung like a votary.

Jem was chatting excitedly away, oblivious to the detachment of his audience. More often he was emphasising his troublesome, almost heroic efforts to secure provisions for his immediate best friend, the responding silence failing to dampen his ebullience.

There was so much to tell and show Terry as part of his induction into his long-term plans as he presupposed, he would be.

"Whoa," he jerked the reigns and sprang abruptly from the cart, faced the hedge and began to pee, still chatting over his shoulder. Feeling the momentary respite in the tension of the straps, the mule took a step toward a dying clump of yellow brown ragwort, tearing at it with its great yellow teeth and scooping up the debris at its feet with great rubbery lips, at the opposing verge.

"Arrhh! Don't let un eat they!" Jem was still trapped in his business and hollered helplessly over his shoulder. Terry afforded him a non-comprehending look.

"Bugger'll be sick if 'ee scoffs that stuff!" Finally finishing his relief, he dashed to snatch the hanging harvest from the great chomping mouth then clambered back up to the cart to flick heavily at the reigns and click his tongue in an encouraging manner that held more hope than expectation as to the mule's cooperation. His worst fears were soon realised with the animal's firm intention to make the most of the intermission.

Uttering an ugly curse, a to familiar problem, Jem retrieved a stout stick from behind the box seat and began to flail at the bony brown hide. A hideous screech of protest in between munches produced the only response.

Broken of his pondering by the scenario, Terry became intrigued. The docile animal looked to prefer a beating than surrender its bounty. Failing in a response from the rear Jem then faced the mule and there ensued a tug o' war with his hands clasped firmly around the huge hairy ears, a red faced and exhausted loser finally conceding defeat with a frustrated kick at the mules rear.

"Git an' move on you bugger!" He continued to cuss while reaching for the birch once more, throwing his weight behind each stroke as if he were beating a carpet slung over a gate, only to succeed in causing the mortality of a few lice. During the fracas, Terry had descended from the cart and leaned laconically against the wooden cartwheel, scratching at the woodworm bores in its rim, amused by the problem in hand, though the onset of cold and the danger of an encounter with a passer-by determined it was time to end this farce.

He scooped a handful of dirty straw from the cart bed and approaching the stubborn beast, knelt beside it to place it onto the road under the mule's belly. Jem stood agog. Evidently still dissatisfied, he then scoured the verge and returned with a small bundle of dry twigs, which joined the other materials in a careful arrangement. The dawning realisation of the plot brought Jem to an apoplexy of delight and disbelief.

From a search in the deep coat pockets, he produced a box of matches which Jem recognised as the one he'd left to ignite the paraffin heater and struck.

"Ha!" Jem hopped in excitement. "Bugger gotta move now!" He broke into a small jig around the mule mockingly imitating its own bray. With the pyre set alight, a thin wisp of grey smoke rose and furled around the swelling belly, until a small flame licked the air, then another until it caught properly. At first oblivious to the danger the mule began to twitch its underbelly in apparent irritation and stamped its hind fore on the spot. The flames grew steadily until both boys took a step back from the stench of burning hair, small sparks ignited the longest hairs and chased them to the root.

It seemed the mule would perish on the spot by its own choosing until it swung its head violently from side to side, let out a pitiful bray that could be heard from some distance, and jumped with its front feet in the air.

Only when its hind legs did likewise, did the burning beast take a step forward in relief. Then another. Jem gave a whoop of delight, hopping about in admiration for the ploy. Terry was a genius to think of something like this!

As the mule moved forward, the pain began to subside, and it came to rest a few yards from its original spot, leaving the now vibrant flames licking the base of the cart.

"Bugger!" Jem froze in mid dance, then sprang into delayed action, flew at the mule and laid into its flank with its big fists. Still the defiant beast decided the punishment was preferable to being on fire and stayed put. The attackers prancing had morphed into a hysterical spin of panic as the farcical dilemma unfolded. He turned with pleading eyes at his companion who had assumed an air of indifference.

The cart smouldered steadily while Jem resumed a fatuous bout with the mule. In desperation he grabbed the britches and traces of the tack, and with fumbling fingers managed to unbuckle the harness. He squeezed himself between mule and cart, heaved mightily backwards and slowly pushed the loaded cart away from the flames, dousing the scorched underside with bare hands, then stamped his heavy boots onto the original pyre. Finally spent, he collapsed onto the road sucking in great gulps of air, the battle won.

His apathetic observer offered a slow handclap as a reward which Jem took as genuine applause, the familiar crooked smile breaking across the flat features. Now his new ally was here there would be plenty of these colourful incidents to provide endless fun for them. It was a portent of how life would be changing, the escapade gave them a shared experience to recall and laugh over in times ahead, there would be many more he was convinced. He spat on his singed palms and scrambled to his feet in a state of mild euphoria.

Amid the scattered debris of his labours, Willie Begg sat squarely on a thinly stuffed sack as a barrier to the cold stone floor, his octogenarian legs spread wide, deft fingers busy in the production of his craft.

He might have been a fisherman painstakingly mending his nets, or a potter working a clay mould on a wheel. In fact, he was a weaver, the withies of the area providing the source for his fine baskets that it was said could be made even to hold water. His delicate thin fingers with gnarled knuckles like knots in a rope were nimbly tucking, folding and bending the prepared sedges that lay at his side.

"That you, Bottle?" The two boys were stood in the doorway of the old stone barn, having to adjust their eyes to peer into the dinginess in which he sat, daylight not penetrating the threshold. Terry had taken a step behind Jem, still unsure of the danger he was exposing himself to.

"Tis, Mr Begg. Got yer peat. I'll just get 'em stacked." He turned to leave Terry fully open to the scrutiny of the weaver whose gaze never settled on him, instead fixed somewhere over his head. Fully exposed for the first time in weeks to the sight of an adult his legs turned weak, not knowing whether to stay or run. Damn that idiot! What was he playing at?

"An' stay away from the house!" Begg shouted.

"I know, Mr Begg."

"Bottle, what's that smell?" He continued to plait the intricate handiwork, ignoring the newcomer's presence entirely. Jem stuck his head around the doorless opening.

"Oh, it's the mule Mr Begg — she caught fire" he disappeared again to leave Terry stripped of his defences.

"Ah, that'll be it then." Begg was satisfied with the explanation. He continued to stare at the old man, who never looked directly at his work or Terry himself, but somewhere in between. Suddenly the penny dropped. With each pinprick of growing recognition amid the darkness he began to see. Because the old weaver couldn't. His opaque eyes were the milky white of his hair, he was blind. A huge sense of relief was tempered by the pique of being made a stooge to Jem's Sally. No wonder he was no threat at all. Even so, he had been teased and did not care for it.

Even then, his annoyance was diluted by the novelty of standing before this man after so many weeks of subterfuge. It felt like being invisible and yet not. A complete unawareness of his presence was a heady power. He took a slow, creeping step forward and peered around at the various finished and half-finished products that lay about, hamper baskets, creels, truckles, and cone shaped fish traps large and small. A fully woven coffin was propped against one wall, that Begg had constructed for himself. A bathtub was filled with withies left to soak. Bundles of the fine stalks were stacked against the other walls, but inevitably his gaze was drawn to the weaver who felt by his side for a length wispiness of the half made basket in his lap, his head cocked to one side like a blackbird on a lawn.

Drinking in the uniqueness of the situation, Terry offered a wave. No response from Begg. He raised his arms and dropped them; the old man wove on. Boldly, and with growing confidence, he pulled a face and extended his tongue. The weaver weaved. Ever more secure in his ability to mock, he raised two fingers to all the old man represented, all the people who had let him down, failed him. Like teasing a gorilla in a zoo, secure behind the bars, he tugged his ears and wagged his fingers. With the silent antics he felt relieved of the frustrations that simmered through all his young years.

When Jem returned, he was stopped short to see the horseplay. Never had he seen such startling impertinence to an adult. Terry had obviously discovered Jem's mild duplicity and was taking full advantage. He looked from one to another in fascination at the insolence. More monkey imitations made it hard for Jem to stifle a giggle. The boy was as daring as he was outrageous and there was no telling what he might do next.

"Finished, Bottle?" Begg was aware of his return. Terry stopped still. "Off yer go then." The boys turned to leave.

"An' Bottle," Begg called after them, "yer frien', he's quite the dancer!"

CHAPTER SIXTEEN

Rolo had been driving in a random circuit of the area for nearly half an hour before he settled on a location, he deemed satisfactory for his purpose. It was a lightly built-up residential area on a road that sloped gently to a junction where the bare outline of a grocer's shop lay at the corner opposite in the failing light of the headlamps. He had cruised along the empty dark roads, where a strictly enforced blackout directive to frustrate enemy bombers discouraged evening footfall. Carefully picking his way at the statutory twenty miles an hour, guided only by the half-covered headlamps that occasionally picked out an occasional white painted lamppost base or length of curb.

After all, road accidents had almost doubled overnight since the orders introduction, where even a struck match or hand torch was frowned upon by an eager A.R.P warden, and recent bombing had only exacerbated the paranoia. Pedestrians collided with one another or were run over by the poorly lit vehicles. One inspired solution by the authorities was a suggestion that a man should be advised to hang out his shirt tail should he be so reckless to venture into the perilous void. Dyed calico curtains prevented any spill of illumination from houses and shops, streetlights were extinguished to produce a ghostly hollowness at dusk. The conditions suited Rolo's purpose entirely. His passenger lay in deep slumber, oblivious of their jaunt and the abuse of his own precious petrol ration, overcome by the infusion of alcohol as he was. Ignorant too, of the fact he had earlier slipped quietly from his barstool into a less than graceful, crumpled heap onto the floor and was helped to his motor by an assisting Rolo who assured onlookers he would take good care of the fellow.

They had stopped at a gentle halt just before the junction and the motor was left running. Alighting from behind the wheel he then walked around to the passenger door and deftly extracted the still dormant Arthur, cradling him in his arms like a baby not to be stirred. Carefully he settled the man behind the wheel, wrinkling his nose at the strong scent of aftershave and gin, then took Arthur's former position beside him. Trusting there was no immediate passer-by in the vicinity, though it was impossible to be certain, he then released the handbrake and allowed the momentum of the slope to ease the motor car forward at a mild pace, where it began to roll across the junction.

"Arthur!" Rolo yelled into the driver's ear, moments before the wheels mounted the kerb and took a heavy jolt into the facade of the grocer's shop with a minor impact, albeit enough to shatter glass and splinter wood. Part of Rolo's calculations considered it would take the proprietors or a curious onlooker in a nearby house a few precious minutes to locate the source of the incident. It wasn't easy for a resident to pull back the curtains in an instant or throw open a door with the blackout materials to content with.

The impact was enough to throw Arthur forward and strike his head on the steering wheel and awaken, though he could make no sense of his circumstances.

"Wha-wha—" was all he could muster, fighting through a fog of confusion. His head hurt, he felt nauseous, a horrible bile in his mouth stung.

"Arthur, we've crashed!" The more he struggled to get a grip on the situation the more his head pounded.

"Wha-wha—" he repeated the plea, recognising at last the steering wheel under his nose, but cognition came like a tricky jigsaw puzzle. He turned to the source of the voice beside him and was baffled when the face of the fellow came into focus. It was pitch black outside the car. It was pitch black inside his head. Worse than the pain, the sickness, even the confusion, was the sense of disorder.

Instinct told him of an event outside of his regimental structure and control, which piled a fear on top of the distress. Crashed? Into what? Where were they? His mouth gaped open, uselessly trying to form a sentence, not knowing where to begin. Rolo was happy to supply the missing pieces.

"You kindly offered me a lift home, remember? To my sister's. Jolly decent of you I must say, but to be honest and truthful, I thought you was a bit worse for wear an' I tried to deter you, but you insisted like the gentleman you be." He allowed the narrative to be digested before carrying on. "I think we've run into a shop, bit o' damage. Hardly your fault in this blackout I would say. Chap doesn't stand a chance." Another pause for the cogs to turn before he released his ace card. "I trust the police will see it that way, I'll certainly be on your side." He allowed a moment for the consequences to sink in though time was limited.

Arthur slapped a palm to his brow, a combination of his numbed forehead and the dawning of his plight, he considered himself thoroughly doomed. Why oh why, couldn't he remember anything?

"Oh dear — oh lord —" he uttered. Rolo wound down a window and listened. No approaching footsteps could be heard, and the shop alarm hadn't activated, it was most likely there wasn't one. Only the mild hissing of the radiator. A placating hand was placed on Arthur's slumped shoulder.

"Come on old chap, it could be worse. No one got hurt. Let's just think a minute." The consoling words were petrol to the flames of Arthur's future. The police. That would mean a court case. Mrs Bolsover-cox. The ministry, the humiliation. It sobered him like a magical elixir.

"Think! Think!" He spat venomously. "I'll tell you what I think! I think I should never have met you! It's your fault, all of it!" The thick vein in his neck began to pulsate again, the pallidness of his face turned red around the dancing pencil moustache. From the fog, flashes of recall were beginning to fight their way through.

"The Kings — the drink — you made me —" Rolo tried to placate, the voice of reason to the growing hysterics.

"Now, now Arthur" he used the name like an old friend. "I don' believe any mention of the Kings Arms would bring you any advantage. Queens be more appropriate I'd say. I fink I'd be correct in assumin' it holds somethin' of a reputation locally for a certain type o' customer, am I right? Now, let's both get some fresh air an' assess the damage." He opened his door to a blast of cold air, leaving Arthur again open mouthed in protest, gasping uselessly for words. Finally he gave up and struggled to vacate his seat. The dizzying rush of evening chill made him grab the shiny black front bumper for balance while Rolo did his best to appraise the harm blindly.

"Motor's not too bad, few dents" he diagnosed. "New shop window for certain. Nuthin' that can't be fixed old chap. Long as the coppers are lenient, I'd say it's not too bad." The mention of the law again, and all it threatened. The giddiness returned; his knees felt weak. Can't be fixed? It wasn't a few dents, it was a huge hollow, a bottomless chasm swallowing his entire standing, all he held dear. Such was his self-pity, the splash of the lifebelt to his drowning went at first unregistered.

Rolo allowed the silence for as long as he dared, then said, "Tell you what, I've an idea. I'll say I was driving." Steadying with one hand on the bonnet, he turned to focus what he thought was the voice of an angel, or more correctly a saint. Were his ears playing tricks? Was it a sick joke? More torment to pile on the agony? He wished to return to the comfort of unconsciousness again. The last sentence was repeated for his benefit.

"You-you—" he stumbled uselessly. Suddenly there was a shaft of light from above, did he really hear correctly?

"Well, when all's said an' done, I do feel partly responsible. I s'pose you'm right in a way. I seemed to 'ave gained a capacity for the stuff over the years, an' you 'ave a lot more at stake than me, what with yer job an' all. To be honest an' truthful, what you see before you is a journey man, wanderin' the avenues of life. The odd pothole is nuthin' to me. I'll take the rap fer this little scrape fer me new friend Arthur."

Arthur grabbed the shoulders of his saviour, more for balance, his gin-soaked breath heavy in Rolo's face.

"I-I don't know what to say. Really, you would do that?" Perhaps there was something of a gentleman in this fellow after all, he had judged too quickly. Everything looked brighter in an instant. There was a get out and it was being offered on a plate. "How-how" he hiccupped, "how can I ever repay you — Raymond?"

"Roland" he corrected, "an' you can stop wrappin' me in your fumes. Tell you what, there might be one small favour you could help with to reimburse the bother that awaits me —"

"Of c-course. How much were you thinking?" Grudging as he would normally to involve himself in any fiscal alliance with a virtual stranger, the situation needed to be resolved quickly before the solution on offer was snatched cruelly away. To be absolved from the mortifying scenario, simply by opening the wallet he was already fumbling for was manna from heaven. Already he had made a mental vow of abstinence from any form of drink and other inclinations for some time.

Rolo pressed a hand on the produced purse.

"Oh — no Arthur, nothing so crass as that, you wound me. I'll tell you what it is. You were tellin' me about your role in the ministry earlier..." Oh dear, did he? Another overdraft in the memory bank, he really must be more careful. That was it, never another drop for as long as he lived.

Rolo set out his proposal, with Arthur increasingly feeling like a frog climbing from a bucket of milk, only to slide back down again. Just when he thought his troubles were over, he felt deeper than ever in the mire.

"Impossible!" Was his indignant reply. "I could never do that! The process must be adhered to!" What this Raymond, or whatever his name was, was asking was a complete affront to his integrity. Oh, how he must have babbled! The man was so well informed of his position in the ministry. Such vetoed conversation would be deeply frowned upon by his superiors, never mind his own principles. Rolo shrugged at his objections.

"Up to you, of course old chap," he said reasonably, "but you'd better decide soon, I think I can hear someone coming." The headache returned with a vengeance.

CHAPTER SEVENTEEN

A frosty cloud of exhaled breath hung over the small herd that wandered the yard aimlessly, driven out from their holding shed for the moment and baying in protest at the delay in the morning feed. Jem was hard at work in scraping out the bedding of their muck filled quarters, painstakingly raking out the fouled straw into the centre aisle where eventually it would be shovelled and borrowed out into a large steaming pile outside the opposing end of the open-ended structure. Sparrows chirped, echoing in the beams as he toiled. Guiltily, he knew recent events had distracted him from the task for too long and now the work was much more laborious. With a large rubber scraper, he pushed the pungent mixture of liquid manure and straw along the floor, occasionally jarring the tool in the cracks and punishing his ribs. Though it stretched his body, his mind was fully occupied elsewhere.

The storyteller was idly sat astride a low dividing wall eyeing the cattle warily. A slack chain prevented them from re-entry, but he still retained a mild fear of the noisy, mud covered beasts. Repulsed too at Jem's stinking task he offered no involvement, though was content to observe, if only to break the monotony of his isolation. Slowly he was gaining the confidence to explore his surroundings at safer times, though the experience left him less than enthusiastic at his discoveries. There was nothing to ignite his interest nor offer any hope for his future.

Jem too had been disappointed at the boy's lack of involvement in the plans he had imagined for themselves, even in the company of Terry, which was sparse and often reticent. Often sulky and easily nettled, he had to tread warily, keen as he was to appease his new friend.

Today though, a lighter more conversant Terry was eager to explain the betterments of an urban life in relation to the farm, his aggrandising was swallowed whole by his enthralled listener who gobbled up the images greedily. By doing so, Jem was unwittingly fanning the flames of the narrator's fancy which even alluded to the family wealth, as was his right. To hear such tales of a life so different to his own in this strange accent was hypnotic to Jem, as was the companionship he cherished.

"…So ya see, soon as I get back, I can send you the money, repay ya like" Terry finished explaining. Jem stopped in his tracks; his train of thought had come off its rails but even then, there was a sense of foreboding.

"Pay?"

"Course," he carried on breezily. Wha'ever you can get I'll pay ya back. You got money in the house ain't ya?' Pronouncing the word house as 'hass'. Still bewildered, Jem shook his head.

"Never seen any" he answered truthfully. Frustrated, Terry hopped down from his perch on the wall, found an area cleared of soiled bedding and walked in slow meditating circles.

"They gotter 'ave some, stan's t'reason" he gestured an arm toward the farmhouse. "'ave a proper butchers will ya?" Still Jem stood in bafflement.

"Wha' for?"

"What for?! What for?!" He was incredulous.

"To get away, you clot! Whad ya fink? Can't do anyfin' wivvout money!" The mood had changed. Terry began pacing irritably. The words had cut like a knife through the air. Even in his very negative moments Jem never imagined, refused to imagine, this scenario. Now it was out, laid bare, his bubble burst.

"You don' wanna bide 'ere then?" Clutching a thread of hope, the words were quietly trembled. A lump began to form in his throat. The statement only served to animate the boy even more. He expanded his arms as if to prove his point, incredulous.

"Stay ere! Effin jokin' ain't ya?! Open yer mincers you ape! What you got 'ere then? Look at it. Might be alright for you an' the rats but it ain't for me! No ta, I'll take me chances somewhere else. Can't be no worse. I don' wanna end up a sodden shit shoveler!" So, there it was. The tirade exposed his intentions all along. Never was he going to play the part Jem had imagined, and in truth he'd never stated he would. This whole time he had been hoodwinking himself and allowing his yearning to fall into the folly of assumption. It had all been for nothing. If the runaway was going to flee again there was nothing to be done. It was akin to damning a stream, or taming a fox cub, the result was inevitable. 'You can't bottle birdsong' Rolo would enigmatically say after one of his long absences. Jem had never really understood. Perhaps now he did.

"Rolo says we're safe 'ere, away from the bombin' says we're lucky" he mumbled feebly into his boots.

"Rolo says — Rolo says, there you go again. 'Oo is this Rolo anyway?" The frustration of failing to raise funds had riled Terry. He became bitter. For some time, he'd seen it as his only realistic chance to move on to something better and now the benign approach had proved fruitless, he was back to square one.

"Ee's my frien' an' we do stuff. Trappin' an' fishin' — all sorts" Jem was affronted at the contemptuous snort of dismissal to his hero.

"He the one wiv that jalopy? I seen 'im — looks like a tinker t'me" he scoffed, but loyally Jem wouldn't concede.

"Well, he's not an 'ee knows everythin'. The younger had had enough of the exchange. Wise as he was to the devotion by Jem of his well-being, the esteem into which this Rolo was held did nothing to manipulate him into being the sole focus of Jem's thoughts and therefore his collaborator. Exasperated, Terry thrust his hands into his borrowed trouser pockets, kicked at the gathered pile and turned to strut away toward the rear entrance, away from the cattle, the piles of manure and the lost solution to his problem.

"There's gotta be somefing 'ere somewhere, somefing worf some money" his voice echoed on departure. For a moment Jem stood and watched him go, his diminishing frame a symbol of Jem's own shrivelled ambitions. He dropped the rake in the silage and followed on, labours temporarily abandoned.

Striding angrily through the twists and turns of the dim, echoing barns and lean-tos that propped each other up like drunken pals. Terry began to rant in frustration at the squalor, waving his arms in a gesture of hopelessness with Jem in tow, fruitlessly trying to placate him with hand movements to quieten. Of course, there was no wealth here, he should have seen that before. The largesse of the house, the outbuildings, the land all an empty shell, dragging these asinine captures into a scratched-out existence no better than his own, quietly accepting their fate as if sat in hells waiting room. The space afforded to them was no more than a hollow sham.

"Me names Jem an' I'm king o' the castle!" Terry loudly mocked on entering a dilapidated barn that appeared the epitome of his ire. It had sucked in the household junk of the years, piles of broken chairs, an upended tattered settee with exploding springs, a

124

doorless wardrobe, picture frames, tea chests filled with broken clocks and single boots, all combining to choke the putrid air with dust and mouse droppings.

Clambering down from the pile and no less determined to pour contempt on what he saw as Jems spiritless beggared life, no better than the one he himself had absconded from, he bitterly chided the bewildered boy. Angrily, he threw open another adjoining timber door, no less convinced it would offer more degradation and underline his derision, to be all at one quietened.

Everything he'd trespassed through till now had been a mausoleum of decay and desertion, dumped into these seedy depressing shacks untouched and unwanted, forgotten until the inevitable march of rust or woodworm claimed them for all time. This was different. It was a place that didn't belong.

He stepped into a long narrow barn, some thirty feet long and fifteen feet wide, outwardly much the same as any other, but this had been converted by someone with an intense purpose. He stood inside a fully fitted workshop, with all the pungency of oily air filling his nostrils. Slowly taking in the layout with widening pupils, this wasn't just any sporadically used shed. It felt alive, busy and breathing, as though the occupant had broken away for a few minutes and was likely to return at any moment to continue his industry. The boys stride slowed to a pace of almost reverence, as he took in the righthand wall in which large casement windows had been carefully cut into the framework for its entire length to attract optimum daylight. Long dead bluebottles piled along its cills. Lacy cobwebs held the dismembered wings of cabbage white butterflies. A startled wood pigeon that had found a way in but not out, flapped noisily in the rafters above.

Against the opposing wall a solid work bench almost as long supported a complete assembly of heavy-duty vices, clamps, buffers, a drill stand and welding equipment. Suspended above, fitted shelves held row upon row of meticulously labelled glass jars filled with nuts, bolts, screws, washers, springs and suchlike.

Wandering along the bench, he allowed his fingers to run over scattered spanners and wrenches, dissembled carburettors, filters and various stripped engine parts in varying states of dismemberment or construction.

"I-I'm not really allowed in 'ere," Jem broke the silence from the doorway, his wavering pleas echoing in the void. "Da always tol' me t'stay out." Though he could sense the boy's angry mood had subdued by this discovery, he was nonetheless nervous at being found here. The entreaty went unheeded. Terry wandered on, looking around as if it were an Aladdin's cave of riches. He picked up an odd tool, replaced it and picked up another, noting each one had the initials W.B inscribed, not just a tool then but a possession of pride and value.

"Oo works 'ere?" A tone of quiet regard had come over the interloper in finding this clearing in the stagnant jungle surrounding him. Held in aspic, it held the enthusiasm and care of someone who might still be present. He wiped his hands on an oily rag.

"No one now, was me uncles I fink, Rolo borrows tools sometimes — we better go." He glanced over his shoulder in worriment Clem should appear, unlikely though it was. The past few weeks had put him through such a gamut of emotions as never experienced before. Terry's varying temperament bringing rise to excitement or exertion, appeasement to anger, never knowing which would be called upon next. At times he felt almost wrung out with the endeavours of his obsession. The plea unheeded, Terry was in awe at his discovery.

On the floor between the bench and the windows, the area was largely taken up with what seemed to be the focus of the work here. It was a strange looking half built contraption which may or may not have started life as a car chassis, now beyond recognition. He circled it warily, trying to figure its purpose. An engine had been fitted to the rear, connecting a toothed driveshaft. A single bucket seat on a low sprung rod protruded from the base, facing a steering handlebar of outsize proportions. Welded solid arms had been fitted to stretch beyond the rear for an unfathomable purpose. It had no wheels, its axles resting high on blocks, but a nearby stack of four outsize steel collars with protruding spikes seemed to fit the bill. It's composite of red, green and base metal colours was testament to its various mixed origins. A string of dusty webs spread over the framework was evidence of the halt in progress from its constructor.

"What is it?" He almost whispered, asking the question to himself. The constructor had been halted in his progress by an event that terminated the project, that was apparent.

"I fink 'ee's dead now —" the sudden rumbling of a diesel engine pulling into the yard bought the explanation to a halt. "Rolo!" Jem was half-relieved at the distraction, half terrified the harbinger was about to be exposed. The very name was becoming a nuisance to Terry, torn to scramble quickly from the fascination of his interest in the contraption and its intention. Even to Jem, under normal circumstances the familiar sound of the engine would be a joyous occasion, a distraction from the mundane and although the arrival had inadvertently succeeded in vacating Terry from the outlawed area, he found himself increasingly muddle headed as to the eventual revelation of his secret since the veil of deceit had begun. Strain and anxiety were becoming familiar bed fellows.

"Go on then!" Terry pushed the frozen figure forward at the call of his name, while he himself scurried rat-like in an opposite direction through the maze, away from the yard. Jem emerged from the barn into the grey daylight with the guilt of reluctance of welcome for his hero, another ailment to suffer. Never before had he welcomed Rolo with less than the esteem of a deity and the contradiction rankled. Just as quickly, it dissipated on the unusual sight before him.

Bound securely with twine of the bulky green bonnet of the truck, its fore and hind legs sprawled either side of the wheel arches was a large and determinedly expired roe deer, splayed as if it had fallen from the sky, which according to Rolo's humble explanation was almost the case.

"Run right in front o' me didn'er. Nowt oi could do, slammed the anchors on but it were too late" he offered remorsefully, raising his trilby to scratch his head with the same hand in ponderous fashion. As only Rolo could do, there was an air of pantomime about his whole performance.   "What to do, what to do, tis a bugger Jem an' that's a fact." He allowed a moment of rumination before continuing.   "Tell 'ee what, no point in wastin' providence, we'll 'ang on fer a week, then divi un up," as though the answer had just struck him, "though lord only knows what yer mother'll make o' her share, we'll probly end up wearin' 'em fer boots!" He bent to untie the trussed deer and pondered.

"Now, where shall us 'ang un? Probly pig shed be best, there's a butcher's hook on the door if I 'member rightly." Jem was almost fit to burst. Right now, he didn't know where Terry had laid low and even if it wasn't the pig shed all the paraphernalia of his tenure was there.

"N-no" he gagged, mind and speech failing to work in unison, the bitter taste of duplicity was becoming too much. Doors too low, 'ee wont hang proper!" Came a sudden burst of inspired explanation. By this time Rolo had the carcass wrapped around his neck like an oversize stole, his head pushed forward, hands gripping his spindly legs for balance. With his restricted view he turned to face his aide.

"Well bugger me if you ain't right, boy. Don' take on so, you'm all of a dither. Go fetch the 'ook an' we'll 'ang un in Two Barn, away frum the cattle."

The rollercoaster of anxiety began its bumpy ride again as Jem ran to the pig barn needing no further encouragement. The sooner the task was done, the sooner Rolo would be on his way, he hoped. An anomaly in itself.

For once the natural warmth and good nature that was as permanent as his battered hat was lost to his devotee. The man whose effervescent rays shone in the darkest corners of his life, whose very presence lightened a load, his absence always a shame on departure, the grin reaper. Now suddenly an encumbrance, almost a villain. A swindler to Jem's preoccupied time, a thief to his loyalties. A torturer to his conscience. Never more so than when faced with his irrepressible friend did the tangled web of deceit tug at his innocent mind. It dried his mouth, cast his eyes downwards, filled his ears and muzzled his head, and here it was again to offer more retribution.

The pig barn was unoccupied as he suspected, Terry not having time to return this far, which only served to raise the blackest fears, the prevalence of doom. Where was he? What if he were holed up in Two Barn? Unslipping the hook from over the door he raced back across the yard, splashing through mud puddles in a desperate attempt to be ahead of Rolo, who he found in mid stride lightly singing, "Come to me, my deerest, let me see thine eyes…"

Jems fears were unfounded. Two Barn, so called for its mirrored construction to its neighbour, was mostly empty. Save a high stack of rotting seed potatoes awaiting long overdue planting that emitted a pungent, earthy, starch waft. The deer was duly impaled from the hook slung over a low beam.

Rolo produced a sharp knife from the ever-present sheath on his belt, and drew the blade across the exposed throat of the animal with a slow deliberate stroke. The once secretive, gracefully noble deer was reduced to a cadaver, its life's blood draining away, its time over.

"Tha's it, git the bucket under. Now, you go an' tell yer ma t' git thit jug on the warm while I finish off. I got some good news fer 'em." Jem turned to obey. He'd hardly spoken, on edge as he was.

"An' Jem — you ain't fed them cows yet I see, don't forget you'm the man o' the 'ouse now, you gotta keep on top of it." Accepting the admonishment, Jem nodded and turned to leave, trying to unravel his confusion. To leave Rolo alone was to fear he might explore the pig shed as he sometimes did to see the birds or borrow a tool from the workshop, unlikely as both were with his preoccupation with the deer. It felt like having a belt tightened by a hole each day, the bitter dishonesty at odds with his nature.

"Rolo," Jem stopped and turned, causing Rolo to turn from his task.

"Nuffin'" he said and moved on. Rolo shook his head. What on earth was the matter with the boy? Steady as a plough horse and reliable as night, he was all at once skittish and distant.

With the door finally creaking closed behind him, Terry crept out from behind the decomposing potato sacks, guided by the day light that crept in from under the slatted door. He stepped toward the animal, awed by the butchery he had witnessed.

There was something hereabouts that reckoned death as routine, and as normal as sunrise, the hanging magpies, the ripped apart swan, the drowned calf, even the old man out in the field for all intents, and now this, whatever it was. An animal he didn't recognise. Some kind of cattle? No, there was a wildness about it, even now. Above his head height a small tail protruded from its hind, to the floor small delicate horns adorned a noble skull. Splayed to its full length never achieved in life, even with the mightiest leap, he braved an exploring

130

hand over its grey-brown hide, taken with its
abrasiveness. Its thin, delicate legs finished with
exquisite hooves, at his feet the handsome head hung
uselessly, the thick tongue lolling for what seemed to be
one last drink. Viscous blood ran freely down over its
face, over the black velvety snout, and dripped steadily
into an already half-filled bucket. Dull black eyes were
unfocused, a fleeting reminder of the blind man. Daring
a feel of a large hairy pointed ear, he found a perfect
round hole behind, the width of his forefinger and sank it
past his knuckle into the skull until it was stopped by
something hard, something metallic.

CHAPTER EIGHTEEN

Clem's recovery was making slow progress over the following week or more, though he did seem buoyed since Rolo's visit with the deer. Not yet able to partake in any form of work, he had however, moved from the parlour isolation to take up his favoured position in the old kitchen armchair, leaving Grace merciful she had one less fire to attend, even then her brother barked wheezing warnings of it's demise. Still swathed in his grubby nightshirt and shawl, his thin chin sprouting a rough grey stubble, he'd even on occasion queried Jem on the general upkeep of the cattle, though still in resentful gruff tones and avoiding eye contact.

How much longer, Jem wondered, before he was about the yard, another liability to worry about. He felt the belt tighten again.

If it wasn't enough to be tormented with the possible discovery of Terry, he began to fret with the boys increasing absence from his nightly domain, a preoccupation that worried Jem to distraction. The dreaded notion his bird had taken flight was unthinkable, and only the disappearance of the daily food procurement offered any comfort, even then entertaining the idea it might have as easily been taken by the rats.

No longer content to hole up in the pig shed like a

pregnant gilt was understandable, although it did nothing to ease Jem's distress at the eventual exposure. At first in denial, he had to concede his own company was surplus to Terry's requirements, the imagined partnership a figment to his heavy heart. If the boy hadn't already gone, it was a matter of time, and if indeed he was still hereabouts, he'd made no effort to make himself known to an anguished Jem who would barely resist calling his name around the farm, instead resorting to desperate glances about for any sign. He was giving everything, for no return, though he'd give even more, for a fraction of friendship.

One morning however, all that changed. His own portion of the previous night's supper of pig's trotters having been deftly secured into the pockets of his ever-worn jacket, (he was now becoming emboldened in the art) he made his casual way through a light, but cold drizzle, with a virtual resignation of the thankless purpose. He might even scoff the meats himself, becoming increasingly hungry after redistributing much of his own food. The lack of gratitude being nothing in comparison to the rejection of his comradeship.

Almost unbelievably, the roughly manufactured bed was occupied and the incumbent soundly asleep. Fervent to establish accord, Jem made a deliberate play of a noisy arrival, upturning the stool with his boot, the clatter echoing off the walls and sending the bullfinch into a fluttering panic.

The unseemly awakening, however, did little to ensure the expected disgruntlement of Terry, who although stirred, was in as placid a countenance as he had ever been, even if clearly lacking sleep for some time.

"Ah Jem, there you are," was the groggy but light welcome. Still clad in the oversize cast offs that made him appear smaller still, he rubbed tired eyes with grubby hands. Whatever he had been up to of late had taken its toll on his time. But it was Jem's turn to feel the fug of the early morning with the unexpected bright reception. The paper wrapped trotters were duly handed over and the grateful boy sat up and swung round to place his socked feet on the floor, breaking a smile in appreciation of the victuals. Through hearty munching he managed,

"Wanted to see ya." With a clearer head Jem might have even acknowledged the first utterance of gratitude bestowed to him for the food, but he was far too preoccupied by this need for his council.

"Siddown," he offered his guest. "I gotta plan an' I need your 'elp." The emphasis on the call for his service was a badge of honour he was proud to wear, all previous forebodings of the absent boy swept away in an instant. Eagerly, he righted the stool and sat before the munching Terry and waited for the unveiling of the plan, determined to appease his friend and strengthen the bond he so desperately sought. If Jem was being so heavily relied upon then the reward of his fraternity would surely follow.

"Well, that ol' blind 'un, you know? I bin finkin," he paused for another bite of the cold meats. With the opening salvo, Jem was instantly deflated once more. Already the conversation had taken a sour tone, this wasn't going to go well, it was obvious.

"I 'member you sayin' 'ee was all on 'is Todd — only im" he added for clarity. "Well, 'ee's got money, must 'ave — sells those fings don't 'ee?" He stopped to allow Jems normally bland expression to try out various facial contortions before it settled on a concentrated frown. Jem begged for the dialogue to take a different course, but his instinct told him otherwise.

"We go over an' see 'im like before, an' you keep 'im talkin' while I take a butchers rand the hass. Tells you to keep away from it, why d'you fink that is? Obvious innit? 'ee's got money in there. Simple." Jem steadied to his feet, slowly backing away as if facing an adder, his mouth agape to find the words.

"I-I—" he stammered.

"I mean, we can do it in broad daylight, won't make no difference, that's the best part" Terry smiled at his ingenuity.

"I-I" Jem tried again, "I don't think I could—" his feeble protest was steamrollered by the masterminds growing enthusiasm for his nefarious scheme.

"Ere's the best bit. I could cut up some paper an' swap it for the money I get. Put the same back, see? Wouldn't know would 'ee? Wouldn't know it was gone. Just countin' newspaper fer pound notes, 'appy as Larry. No reason to call the coppers!" He allowed himself a chortle at his cunning and sat back to await the praise no doubt owed. For Jem, the image of the old man counting pieces of newspaper for one ridiculous moment reminded him of the china eggs he'd put under the broody hens a few minutes before. But if he thought he'd suffered a torment of emotions before, this was a complete maelstrom. He doubted he could take more of this. The conflict between his own moral values and the urge to appease his friend. For a second there was almost a wish to go back to a time before the boy and his destructive ways, a time before all the lies and deceit to his elders that wrestled so uneasily on his conscience. With Terry's discovery, he'd imagined a future of brotherhood and shared experiences, of fun and bonding, naively assuming a character much like his own, of hard work with the shared joy of each season's offerings. Instead, it had been nothing but skulduggery, of craven stealth, of mendacious hoodwinking. It had taken a life of its own, unstoppable. And now his would-be ally was proposing daylight robbery to his ailing neighbour. He took another step back as if to distance himself from the whole shoddy business, shaking his head in lieu of the words that wouldn't come.

"What, you not gonna 'elp me?" Recognising the resistance, Terry's mood instantly changed.

"Fat lot a good, you are" he spat bitterly, "say

you want to see me right, but when it comes to it... Same as all the rest — no odds, I'll do it meself — don' need you." He tossed the scraps of meat on the floor in a gesture of reflection and stared moodily at them to indicate the conversation was ended. The silence was heavy.

"I do want t 'elp you, I do" Jem softly protested "it's just — well I never —" he balled his fists in frustration, searching to prove his good intent, continuing to suffer the punishment of disregard inflicted on his wracked mind. Invited into the confines of the conspiracy, he'd found himself with the sting of rejection again. Out of favour, he needed to repair the damage quickly.

He crossed the floor and reached high on the bullfinch cage, carefully lifting down an old wooden cigar box, carrying it across to the sulking boy who still bored his eyes to the floor. Wordlessly Jem reached out to place the box before his gaze. Terry looked up and slowly took the offering, placing it on his lap, surprised at the weightiness, and stared at the fading paper label on the lid that depicted a sombre hawk nosed Red Indian Chief in full headdress. The hinged lid was slowly opened like a music box, the contents scrutinised. He reached in and rummaged with a grubby hand; Jem awaited the reaction with bated breath. The tiny metals tinkled and jangled as Terry lifted them and poured them back into the box between his fingers like a pirate opening a treasure chest.

"Tanners!" He exploded. "Soddin' tanners!" The box was thrown to the floor whereupon a few score sixpences and the odd shilling crashed and rolled around noisily, setting the bullfinch off in distressing flutters.

"What am I sposed to do wiv tanners weighing me down! I wus talkin about proper money, not loose change!" Jem stood mortified. His only real possession, the profits of his bird sales to Rolo gathered slowly over time, some as shiny as jewels, some dull, as if of a different value, scattered and strewn like worthless scrap. Some still rolled in random directions, until falling silent to the black mood that prevailed. A mutual despondency settled on the two. Jem stepped a heavy boot over the once coveted silver to leave, revered not for its value but for what it represented in his relationship with his business partner. They crunched underfoot. He opened the door and walked out into the light drizzle with the heavy heart he had arrived with. The fantasy had all gone so wrong, nothing like his dream of the future. Like the pull of gravity, he was drawn into the boy's orbit but now began to see they belonged to different worlds. They were further apart than ever.

If Terry's scorn hadn't been enough, he plunged a further knife into Jem's heart as he walked out, with a comment. A revealing truth that left him spinning with confusion and deliberation for the rest of his long, miserable day.

Persistent rain, sharp and cold gathered in great puddles across the yard, broken guttering created small glugging waterfalls that channelled into the puddles from hundreds of small, veined rivulets.

The lorry wheels splashed to a screeching stop when its half-masked headlights picked out a distressed and bedraggled Grace through the blackness, her hair matted with the wet, odd strands plastered to her face and an old raincoat thrown over her shoulders, clutched at the neck. Her sodden condition made it apparent she had been out for some time.

"Why Gracie girl, what's doin' out old girl? You'll ketch yer death," Rolo stuck his head out of the lorry window and hollered above the noisy downpour. "I jus' come up to divi up thit venison, honest and truthful, the boys bin swillin' well down the Feathers tonight an' thats the best time to ketch em, should fetch a good —"

"Ohh Roly!" she clutched at his arm desperately.

"It's Clem, he's gone — disappeared!" For once lucid, through terrified, Rolo quickly disembarked while she explained in a fervour how she'd retired early, leaving her brother dozing by the dying embers. Then, disturbed by the back door banging in the wind, she returned to find him gone. Rolo released his hands from her begging grasp, put a reassuring arm around her shivering shoulders and steered her back toward the kitchen steps.

"Now Gracie, you'm al of a dither, on you go an' get thit fire built up again, an' dry yerself, I'll find the old fool, ee can't 'ave gone far." Grabbing a rainproof coat and torch from the cab, he threw it over his head and began the search. The rains illumination in the torch magnified its severity but Rolo could only hope the man was under shelter and headed for the complex of barns, calling out at intervals. Rain fell steadily on the tin roofs, any muffled reply difficult to detect. What on earth made the man leave the house at this hour, and in his condition? On the mend he might be alright, but exposure in this dirty night could be the end of him. It was a fruitless search at first, difficult enough with the obstacles of the building's contents. Repeatedly, shadows tricked him into a false sense of success, only to be frustrated again. He searched the hay barn, the cow parlour, Two Barn, and was flashing the light around the cider barrel store to no avail. Perhaps the pig shed might be worth a look. He became exasperated. It was then a small, but unmistakably soft weeping came from the small cow stall in a dark corner.

"Clemmie old cock, that you?" He approached the noise warily. The weeping was pitiful, like the whimper of a dying animal. Soon enough the torchlight picked out the bent old frame, sat huddled in his shawl. Rolo squat on his haunches beside the sorrowful figure who slowly looked up distraught, tears wetting his crumpled face in the glow of the torch. He seemed to be staring into an abyss his mind elsewhere. He whispered, almost to himself.

"Tis Will, he's back!"

"Wha's talkin' about ol' feller? Wha's doin' out?" He thought Clem had finally lost all reason, his malady far graver than at first suspected. Much the same way in which his sister had clasped Rolo's leather strapped wrist, so too did the broken man. He turned to Rolo.

"eared an ingine — frum the workshop you know — came t' see. I opened the door — 'ee pushed right past me in the dark — a ghost — pushed me over.!" He began to sob again. Rolo pressed a hand on his bony shoulder.

"Now see 'ere Clemmy, you not bin well an' —" Clem carried on unhearing.

"Never spoke — Will I says, it's me — but ee keep on running, it wuz 'im alright. Always tinkerin' in thit shed — wouldn't speak t' me —" he bowed his head mournfully "ashamed o' me I 'spose." He broke down again.

Familiar as Rolo was with the workshop and its provenance, and indeed the fate of the siblings as once relayed by Grace many years before, he was no less sceptical of Clem's ramblings.

"C'mon now Clem, tis yer own fool mind playin' tricks on 'ee, you bin ill an' you ain't right still, let's get ee back in the house an' warmed up." He heaved the fragile frame with ease and supported his weight once again across the yard, through the ever-growing puddles, with Clem still muttering incoherently.

Eventually the haunted man was resettled in his familiar armchair, Grace fluttering around him in relief. Under a weak breath he repeated his call to Will, begging forgiveness.

Rolo left them alone to execute his original purpose, once again venturing across the yard en route to the deer in Two Barn. For a moment he glanced across to the barn in which lay the workshop, the cause of Clem's angst and the place of his vision. Ghosts indeed, Rolo thought, what had gotten the old man into this state? The whole place was falling apart as it was, without this.

Of all the anguished filled nights of late suffered by Jem, this was by far the worst. Lying awake in the darkness, the candle long expired, under the itching coarse blanket, he too was being haunted by a voice. It was that of Terry's and the parting tease that at first he dismissed, then slowly as the day grew, so did the likely truth of his comment.

"He lets 'em go, you know, those birds. No different to what I did really. I seen him wiv me own eyes, out by the wood one night. Didn't know who he was then, thought it was queer. Fetches a cage from out that van of 'is full o' birds, talks to them a bit an' opens the door an' off they go, probably tellin' 'em what a mug you are! He finished with a snort. It couldn't be true — and yet. The words echoed again and again.

Drifting up the bare wooden stairs and into the relative bareness of his bedroom, a mild commotion seemed to be happening at this late hour, his mother's shrill voice, and the familiar deep baritone of Rolo's. The voice that had previously been a rich gurgle of humour and wisdom, reassurance and dependence, that spent time with him, that asked Jem his thoughts, encouraged him. His only true friend. His partner in their alliance to sell the birds. All the time Rolo was throwing a stick for him to fetch and drop at his master's feet, tail wagging for the silver pat on the head. He never wanted the birds to sell on. The Linnets and Siskins, Bullfinches and Goldfinches he'd spent hour after hour stalking and capturing in his eagerness to provide his end of the bargain. All the time Rolo was in pretence with his gratitude and patronising payments, why did he do it? Was it a mere eccentricity that amused him? A contrivance for Jem to have money of his own, why? The questions never ceased. What else was there about Rolo that he'd accepted without question? Even the mule he'd provided without explanation, his disappearances, suddenly everything about the man, everything Jem had built him up to be, was unreliable. Whilst he had tormented himself for being less than honest for the first time with Rolo, the man was carrying a furtiveness of his own. While all the time berating himself to feel ashamed of his deceit, his friend was doing it with a smile.

The box of sixpences meant nothing to him now, no more than it did to Terry. It was tainted. And what of Terry? Drifting further away from the chum he hoped for, a dark side that Jem didn't understand, nor wish to be dragged into. There was underhandedness all about, even contributing to it himself. As the voices carried on from downstairs, he buried his head under the blanket, feeling more isolated than ever.

CHAPTER NINETEEN

It was becoming near desperation now, the options virtually non-existent. For weeks, the sanctuary of the farm had sustained him, kept him alive from the elements, but it offered nothing for his future. He had no desire to continue to be a covert pet of the simpleton who's fawning sycophancy was becoming a nuisance.

Weighing the risk before deciding on its worth, he gingerly mounted the wooden steps before trying the door handle. It opened, no going back. He slipped in and pulled it quietly shut. The Charabanc had been parked in the yard for some time, its headlights illuminating the rain sodden yard, drawing him like a beacon. It had been a near thing, the old man turning up like that and he could only trust the resulting mild commotion in the house would carry on long enough for his purpose. The total blackness inside made it difficult to make any sense of the layout and striking a match was the only option, quickly drawing curtains that dressed the windows.

The stark flare revealed a basic but somehow snug domicile, all space optimised for maximum containment like a ship's galley. There was a narrow but long pull-down bed, tight fitting cupboard space, a small stove and other fitments. For a moment he held a sense of mild admiration for the self-contained home on wheels, able to travel wherever, whenever. Fishing rods were cleverly clipped over his head to the roof, even a small bookshelf was accommodated, prevented from spillage by a movable bar. But there was little time for admiration, where to begin the search? A small two drawer chest at the foot of the bed, seemed most likely, though the top drawer yielded nothing of value. In the second with another match, he rummaged a jumble of penknives, tobacco, a broken watch, some string and such sundries, that rested upon what looked like a brown cardboard, official looking file with a ministry crest on its cover. Underneath that, two small sepia photographs, one of a young woman coyly looking at the lens, obviously reluctant to pose. The other of a baby in a box crib, ugly as all babies were to him, though with its disproportionate ears this one abused the privilege. All of no interest. A fumble to the back of the drawer and his ferreting fingers closed on what felt like a tubular bundle which he withdrew into the light. It was a roll of tightly bound paper in an elastic band. White paper. He removed the band and opened the bundle. Five-pound notes! He slumped on the bed in disbelief. Of all the finds! More than he'd ever seen, a hundred pounds, maybe more! The possibilities were too much to contemplate.

Almost numb to the senses with the prospects of the fortune, it was a crippling moment before he registered the shifting of the weight to the front of the vehicle, and a shockingly fierce vibration that shook the pots and pans into a noisy crescendo from hooks hung over the stove. A loud bang of backfiring and heavy revving later, he was thrown to the floor from a sudden jerk.   'Soddin'ell!' His mind screamed; they were moving! The match was snuffed out and the giddiness of his new fortune left him stunned into non-action before the truck lurched from reverse to forward with a crunching gear change — trapped! Oh, wretched misery piled upon wretched misery. What else could the fates do

143

to compound his misfortune, every step forward took him closer to another brick wall. By the time the wash of self-pity had receded and he located the door in the darkness, the increasing speed discounted a desperate leaping out as an option.

Swaying from side to side through the lanes, he was forced to sit on the bed for balance, only the heavy drape saving him from the impending disaster of discovery by this reckless driver. Just a few feet away on the other side of the curtain, as close to an elder as he had been for a number of weeks, was he about to be exposed after all? There was nothing to be done but sit it out and wait for the speed to drop enough to make a lunge for freedom again. But how far was it likely to go? It might be mile after mile. The rush of excitement suddenly brought with the wealth in his tightly clutched fist encouraged a light headedness that began to amuse, after all they were travelling away from the farm. Maybe not so much a predicament after all, more a slice of good fortune only just recognised, money and travel, he had it all! Ha! Longing to see the riches again with his own eyes, not just to feel the thick wad, he pondered the next move. Perhaps they'd even go as far as Bristol or beyond. He could only speculate, even with some facetiousness. 'I say driver, London please and step on it' imagining peeling off a note from the roll and waiving it under the nose of his innocent abetter through the drape. The constant swaying told him they were still negotiating the winding lanes, it was possible they would trundle through the night, though he suspected they hadn't gone that far yet. Part of him wanted to be off now, to begin a new start with the enormous bonus. Conversely, the longer he stayed put, the sooner he would be putting distance from the farm.

A sudden slamming of the brakes and a piercing screech of the tyres threw him off the bed and crashing to the floor with a violent jerk. The muffled thump of knees and elbows on the carpeted floor was drowned by the curse of the voice behind the drape.

"Bugger ee, badger!" In saving himself from the impact and an instinct to spread his hands, the money spilled out and rolled away agonisingly from his despairing reach. Pots and pans settled their clanking, the gears crunched to engage again, and they were moving. The opportunity to bail out had gone, as was the will with the money dropped. Frantically, he groped blindly under the bed and all around, feeling only emptiness and dust. His stomach felt nauseous at the panic to retrieve the golden opportunity, but no matter how much he scrabbled around there was nothing to replace that wondrous shape and feel, the certainty of better times of only a minute ago.

Once again, the fates had conspired to inflict their cruellest taunt yet, elation had turned to dread, chance to misfortune as quickly as it teased. How much more bad luck was his due? The money was everything, the one chance to start a fresh. To be safe, secure, it was everything. He must find it. But rising anger and desperation blurred any structured inch by inch search, instead a panicky clawing of thin air, the wretchedness of loss promoting nothing more than a wild rummage. It was hopeless, and as if it couldn't get any worse, he sensed the truck slowing, the engine quietening, the gears changing down. It was preparing to stop. They hadn't gone far at all, maybe two miles. He stretched up to chance a peak behind the small window curtain, scattered rooftops outlined against a weak moonlight. It had to be the nearest village. Which meant people. Which meant trouble. Decision time. To make a break for freedom, if thats what it was? To leave behind the one chance in his life to change it forever? Or to run and prolong the hiding, scrounging scraps, always looking over his shoulder. To live in a netherworld, subversive and destitute. But to risk staying to recover the cash and getting caught? Being handed over to the authorities, go back to start, do not pass go, do not collect two hundred pounds.

The cab lurched as the driver's door opened and a weight alighted. It was the proverbial monkey with its hand stuck in a jar with a handful of peanuts. Let go, it was the only answer. He burst through the rear door, clearing the steps with a leap and landed on the hard road, breaking to a run without looking back. A holler chased behind him.

"Hoi, what's up there?!" Within yards the night swallowed him up, running yet again.

CHAPTER TWENTY

Bolsover-Cox drummed his fingers in agitation on the highly polished desk, crunching a peppermint so aggressively it was a though his pencil moustache had a job to hang on to his dancing top lip. The sound in the otherwise hushed office carried to a subordinate who kept his head down. He recognised the warning sign, and it wasn't good. Arthur was a sucker, not a cruncher. Unable to focus on the mounting paperwork before him, partly in frustration, but mostly with seething anger, he had come to the conclusion he had been duped, taken for a ride, rummied or whatever the phrase was these days, and he didn't care for it, not one little bit.

The whole sorry episode had been haunting him for days, parts still missing, some linking some not, like a jigsaw puzzle. And now after much scrabbling through his overworked cerebral he was sure the final piece had fallen into place and it wasn't a pretty picture.

He cringed at the vague memory of the police constable who arrived on foot and taking in the lack of sobriety of the pair, cautioned the confessed driver with a lack of due care and attention and damage to the property. As good as his word, Rolo steadily accepted the charges and the two were allowed, groggily in one case, to find the nearest taxi rank a few streets away, with Rolo fully understanding the matter of law would take its course. It was sometime late into the evening when Arthur arrived sheepishly home minus one motor car and the beginnings of a monstrous headache, notwithstanding the deep consternation of his spouse. As far as he was concerned it was the last he wanted to see of the wretched man, but it didn't end there.

It was Arthur's turn to keep his end of the bargain, which rankled deeply. He had been reluctantly 'coerced' as he saw it now to hand over the item of the swine's interest, it being the desperation of his confused state and avoid the attention of the law that he ceded. A neutral venue was agreed, after the blighter's initial suggestion they should conduct the affair at the King's Arms was robustly refused by Arthur, who had no desire to frequent the establishment for some time, before he erased the memory of a man of his standing should be carried out. A large crunch of peppermint. A piece went down the wrong way, he almost choked.

Still more than that. It was something that gnawed away at the whole chapter of events. It began when he was finally able to reunite with his motorcar from the garage, (having to take a bus of all things!) he duly and thankfully sank into the familiar seat, pulled it forward to reach the pedals and started the engine. The equilibrium was re-established. But wait. There it was! He'd had to re-adjust the seat. Why? Because somebody else had been driving! That was the missing piece! That-that oaf was driving all the time! Unprovable but nevertheless fact. The whole thing was a total contrivance from the very beginning. It all fitted now. The scoundrel's improbable appearance at the Kings, the bonhomie, the plied drinking. Arthur had been taken in hook, line and sinker. And worse. Against his principles he'd been constrained into an agreement to hand over a precious ministry document, with all the surreptitious treason it entailed. It jarred against his morals; it wasn't on.

Having realised the whole scenario for what it was, he was singularly determined to gain the upper hand over that rascal (he'd forgotten the man's name) who would pay dearly. Nobody makes a monkey of a Bolsover-Cox. As it was, his extremely cautious nature ordained he should make a copy of the file and in doing so, to resurrect it to its fullest conclusion would now be a priority. But still it wasn't enough. What to do about the blaggard himself?

By the very fact it had so recently been at his attention he knew the case by heart. Bottle was the unforgettable name, as was the dreaded farm and the land appertaining to it. But what was the blighters interest? Probably related somehow as they all were, he scoffed silently, inbreeding was rife wasn't it, in the sticks? Mmmm. There was the court case of course. He would get his comeuppance there. Due justice would take its course surely. But the duplicity would still go unpunished. And what if he absconded, being the type that he was. More pondering. The court case. A sudden jolt of remembrance.

Among his (dear) wife's admonishments as he departed, was a reminder not to be late that evening as she was hosting one of her intolerable bridge nights. Though usually this news would be met with less than enthusiasm, he was suddenly reminded of a recent new member of his wife's ever-growing entourage. A rather handsome young fellow with an unfortunate propensity to stutter.

Arthur had paid his usual indifferent attention to the conversation during the course of the previous gathering, but now one thing came to mind that could be suddenly significant. The fellow of his now renewed interest was on the bench of the local magistrate's court. He pondered some more, mmmm. She must invite him. He popped another peppermint into his mouth and began to suck.

It had been raining through the night and as a grey wash settled over the dawn it now turned to a fine drizzle. The kind of trifling droplets that would seep into clothes and hair without a person acknowledging they were wet through. Certainly, Jem was oblivious to it. At least it had softened the ground and made the grave easier to dig.

Between bad tempered thrusts of the spade his mood darkened to that of the earth he disturbed. So, this was how it was going to be. Plodding along in this solitary furrow. For all his best endeavours he was bound to continue in the same old way, no one for company, at times not uttering a spoken word for a whole day. Not consciously considered before but having sampled the promised sweet taste of an exotic fruit, it was nothing more than a rank tang of bitterness, like finding half a maggot in a juicy apple. The remoteness of his father and his ill-tempered manner, his mother would have coherent moments, but they were becoming fewer, fighting with her jumbled mind. A brown world, the same old picture. A brown, black canvas the colour of peat, heavily framed that no light should penetrate.

Then there was Rolo. The only splash of colour who broke through the scene with his sky-blue persona. Enough blue to make a sailor a pair of trousers, he would say at a breaking sky. Rolo who turned out to be tainted. Deceiving him with a necessity for the birds he never really wanted. Reminded of the pride whenever he provided the man with a cache of the songbirds and Rolo's apparent delight, he felt a prick of embarrassment at his own gullible trust. Rolo, now painted grey.

…And Terry. What of him. All at one changing the whole picture and the subject matter. Breaking the composition of the landscape. But now it was never going to be the image of his fancy. Fooled again and being made the fool again. Though he had to admit at last, how he'd pretended to himself the boy would settle here, and with his increasingly difficult ways, Jem finally accepted he didn't belong in the scene. It was an awkward fit. Terry painted out of the whole uninspiring bucolic picture.

He stood inside the roughly shaped hole and dug some more. Knee height. It wasn't deep enough yet.

"Dead then". Deep in his own examination of self-pity, he never heard the approach, the surprise making him correct himself from his natural delight at the rich voice. Jem turned, and there he stood. Pulled up shirtsleeves, brown corduroy trousers, the familiar waistcoat and the warm smile. Same as always. Except he wasn't. He was a trickster, a pretender not to be trusted. Keen to avoid eye contact, Jem turned his back and dug with renewed vigour, the steel of the spade slicing into the earth. At the side of the hole the old cur lay in a wooden wheelbarrow, its head hanging over the side, awaiting its final resting place and relieved at last of its tortuous malady. Its mangled fur was curled into small knots from the rain. Jem tried a grunt of confirmation, but it stuck in his throat, his chest constricted with the effect of treating his hero with indifference.

"Wheres 'ee to then?" Rolo spoke softly, unaccusingly, a mild enquiry. Still Jem refused to address him properly, half afraid he would buckle under the anomaly of rebuffing the man.

"Who?" He choked, still digging with farrow. The hole was deep enough but he kept going, his head level with Rolo's knees.

"The boy, Jem. The one you bin 'arbourin'" it was too much. He could resist no more. A sudden release to heave his deception exposed at last. He stopped digging and turned to look up. Rolo continued.

"Oh, I've known fer a while, me old cock. Jus' come frum the pig shed. Ain't interfered, not my business. Twas obvious really what wi your actin' all furtive lately, even yer mam wonderin' why you'm eatin' fer two." Jem was taken aback.

"Oh ah Jem, she ain't lost all 'er buttons yet. You ain't cut out to be a dodger boy, you got yer 'onesty, don' change that old chap." He couldn't help it, the accusation blurted out with all the frustration of his mulling.

"Like you, you mean?" There it was, out. "Wiv the birds, lettin' 'em go all the time. Clot I were, probly catchin' the same ones over again!" The outburst was followed by a silence as Jem tried to control his breathing, until Rolo crouched to match him at head height. He pulled a roll up from behind his ear but made no attempt to light it, content to keep rolling in between thumb and forefinger.

"Ahh, so that's what tis! Well, I spose the lad told ee that. Well, if 'ee looks at it like that, a bigger fool oi fer payin' fer me own birds over an' again! Now look 'ere lad, there's a bigger picture 'ere. See, they ain't gettin' any younger." He thumbed over his shoulder to the direction of the farm.   "One day you'm gonna be runnin' this place an' sooner'n you think. But its gunner be hard Jem, an' you need to change things round, specially with this war on. You'm gon 'ave to 'ave a lot of patience, when things don't go right. An' guile, a little bit of imagination an' cunnin', specially with the ministry on yer back." Jem frowned in puzzlement. "Well, that's fer another time, ferget it fer now. Honest an' truthful, I didn't want 'em no, but I wanted 'ee t' learn patience an' cunnin' frum all they hours out catchin'." Jem found his resistance ebbing. Rolo's soft tones was a balm to his inner turmoil but as a last fight to remain objectionable, he protested feebly.

"But I can't do it on me own!" Rolo held up a large palm to continue.

"Well, when 'ee looks at it, you already 'ave priddy much. Now, 'ere's the thing. There's a lad or two in the village runs odd jobs fer me sometimes, sells rabbits fer me an' stuff. Good sorts, willin' to learn. A little bit of help 'ere an' there, wi you showin' 'em the ropes, be 'appy to give hand here an there fer the odd tanner or two. 'Ventually, when you'm up an' runnin' proper, you can take un on full time." The words slowly sank in, with Jem pulling a gamut of expressions as he wrestled with the pros and cons. Once more under the spell of Rolo's words he so much wanted to believe. Did he really mean it? Working with a lad of his own age? Being the master — paymaster even? There was an echo of familiarity with these thoughts he'd had of late, but on hearing them spoken from Rolo, there was practical realism. The subliminal yearning had been put into words, he wanted to hear more, much more.

"This boy," he encouraged "he'd do it, really?" Wanting so much for Rolo to expand on the idea. The drizzle stopped, a beam of sun broke through, or so he might have imagined.

"I'll sort it, don' worry. First things first. Now, where's 'ee to Jem, any ideas? You know it can't carry on like tis, time t' get it sorted." All at once, glad to relieve himself of the burden, he sat heavily to the edge of the hole and blurted.

"I dunno. I left 'is scoff out las' night an' it was still there this mornin. Gone missin' a lot lately but always has his grub. Gone fer good I 'spose this time — I was only tryin' to 'elp him." He finished feebly. How strange it sounded now to be talking openly of the guilty concealment and how much better he felt for it. No more of his shame and deception. It was a burden lifted, a weight he thought to carry alone, underestimating the toll on his natural honesty and innocent.

"Willie Beggs — 'ee talked of robbin' 'im t' get some money. 'ow easy it would be —'ee came wiv me once to deliver sum peat once." Again, he tapered off with a little shame at his previous slight. The confessional came with its own mixed bag of chagrin and naivety, good as it was to be rid of the load.

"Strewth." Rolo tipped his hat back a touch."'ow

153

much more does 'ee want?" More puzzlement from Jem, "never mind lad, oh well, 'ee don' know about — I bedder get over there quick." He stood to take his retreat back across the field.

"What? What is it?" Jem called.

"No time now, gotta go."

"Shall I come?" Eager to join Rolo again in whatever he was about, taking a step out of the hole. But Rolo called back over his shoulder.

"Best finish off 'ere, I got enough heads to stick back on." He watched the man walk hurriedly away. What did he mean? What was so perilous at Beggs to make Rolo for once deeply concerned? Whatever, he would sort it. Rolo would always make things right. Rolo, his hero. Rolo who was going to sort him with some help from the village. He leant on the spade watching the figure disappear, lost again in plans for a lad under his tutelage to help with the load, to break the solitary path. The cur lay in the barrow, having to wait a little longer for its final resting place.

CHAPTER TWENTY ONE

The door lintel was low, therefore the wooden door itself oddly slight for adult use. Long peeled away varnish allowed the sun to bleach the panels to a pale grey. A single small bullseye pane revealed nothing from inside with its whirled contortions. No letterbox, a back door. A simple door with a brass knob handle to open inwards. Only a door. But somehow it was the culmination of all he had become of late. To enter would be the fork in the road, his most audacious, desperate act yet. A second attempt at larceny in the space of a day. The representation of the wretchedness of recent weeks. After this, he determined never to be driven to this again. Justification was easy. When things turned more favourable, any gains could be repaid in time, his need was greater, what the old man didn't miss wouldn't hurt him. All that talk of swapping money for paper, well that was just showing Jem of his artfulness.

Through the night he'd wandered in random circles trying to keep warm. His body ached for sleep, for more nourishment, but now they would have to wait. As the dawn broke, some by now familiar landmarks began to emerge. The tor to the east, an odd church spire, the old bridge that he'd once slept under, so long ago it seemed, and not progressed since. And then, the road once travelled to Willie Beggs' abode, as though it was laid out to guide him. Having once clutched a small fortune in his small first, the euphoric upsurge in his options insisted it was the only way out. Money had the power to decide, rather than be decided upon. The desperation and weariness of his entire being brought an almost irrelevance to the consequences, but then again, what could go wrong? As the mulling of his conscience turned, so did the loose brass knob that filled his trembling hand.

Taking a deep breath, he put a tentative step over the threshold and onto the cold flagstone floor. Silence. The old man must be working out in the shed. The back door was left open for a quick escape, should the need arise. He strained for the slightest sound. Somewhere, a ticking like a clock somewhere. Daylight chased in behind him, like water keen to rush forward. A kitchen, sparse, cold. A single small table and one chair in the centre. A singular window over a sink, its curtains drawn, as he assumed they were permanently, daylight was surplus. A large stone sink, a lightly dripping tap proving the source of the ticking sound, measuring time. Still on the spot, he surveyed the layout. An internal door opposite, slightly ajar, a parlour most likely. Cupboards ran along on wall, a chest with some drawers. It felt barely lived in. Where to begin? He tiptoed further into the cold mustiness of the room toward the drawers, which squeaked a little with the pulling. Nothing there, some cutlery, linen, mediocre oddments. A wall mounted cupboard above. The door opened. A plate, some cups, a half loaf of bread. A sudden flash of movement, he froze. It dashed toward him, flew from the open door, landed on the worktop and scurried away. A mouse. A sigh of relief. For all the simplicity of the act, he was becoming less confident, more unsure, of what he was doing. The kitchen was going to yield nothing. It was becoming obvious. People didn't keep valuables in the kitchen, it had to be the parlour. Dare he venture into the dark recess of the house? With each careful step deeper still into the repercussions if it went wrong. Not only that. It was one thing to devise a ploy to take money from the old man, feeble and vulnerable as he was, but it was beginning to gnaw at his conscience. Is this really what he had come to? Was this the only way? As yet, his crimes had been petty, harmless, but as the parlour door drew him across the room into the shadows, he almost felt lured into a darker vision of his own fate.

To be away from this godforsaken land was paramount no doubt, but here, stood in another's house, searching to steal another's possessions, suddenly brought home the baseness of his existence. This act wasn't escaping from that, it was compounding it. Vindication was seeping away as every moment, measured by the dripping tap, passed. Go. Go now. Find another way. There was a smell, a rank odour like bad breath, stale and somehow ominous. Something wasn't right and not only his presence here. A kitchen door was ajar behind, allowing a pool of daylight on the floor, the parlour door ahead, an open portal of temptation. Half the kitchen plunged into a murky dimness. Then something else. Something deep and throbbing like a rumble of distant thunder, low at first, barely audible, but growing more intense until it began to fill his ears and prickle his skin. It had no source or direction but filled the air with a slowly building crescendo. The echo bounced around the room, ricocheted off the walls, swamped his senses. It became thunderous. There was nothing to see, only to feel the vibration that might as well have risen from the bottom of a mineshaft. The threat was overpowering, the growl deafening. Run! He unlocked his rooted legs. Too late, he was thrown to the floor by a weight so oppressive it knocked the air from his lungs. An attack. A huge snarling beast bore down, pinning him to the cold flagstones, much heavier than himself and snapping the air with viciously strong, drooling jaws that bared needle sharp fangs. With a momentary pause of pressure as it shifted its position in order to gain better purchase, he rolled to face upward at his attacker, to stare at maddened red eyes berserk from bloodlust, that pierced down from a thick, black face and heavy skull. It's entire head twice the size of the boy's own, and a heftily muscled body that overwhelmed him.

Still snapping and lunging, its bear like paws pressed down on his thin chest, it pinned him down to utter hopelessness. With another snarling pounce, the brute took a bite at the boy's shoulder, sank its teeth through his jacket. Having gained a vice like grip, it shook him from side to side like a rag doll. His brain was rattled into semi-coherence, the violent tossing blacking out all sense from his terrified being, while the great beast roared its deep guttural gnarling with the intensity of a hell hound juddering through its mass of fur. Blood began to trickle from the shoulder wound and seeped outward onto the tweed jacket. The devil dog never let up in its murderous intent, with no air in his lungs to scream out, beginning to blackout with the violent rattling and excruciating pain from the bite. On the onslaught went. Ear splitting growling never abated, filling the room with its odious intention. Pathetically, he pressed weakened arms into the enormous hairy chest to repel it, the suffocating heaviness all consuming.

Relentlessly the attack went on, the fervour animal determined to shake the last breath from its victim. As the chaotic frenzy went on, so did the boy's body become limp and unresisting. The roaring growl took on a higher pitched yelp, as though the beast itself was feeling its own pain, though it never yielded any pressure on its grip nor ceased its manic shaking. From nowhere two strong hands had a grip on each large, black ear and yanked at the bullhead, driving the animal into a more agonised fury, but the hands held on tightly. The tug-o-war continued for what seemed like an eternity. The rescuer felt the pains of his arms being pulled from their sockets, wearing with the strain. It was like riding a bull, he daren't let go. Berserk with the indignity of suffering its own attack, it released its grip on the limp body and snapped wildly behind its back at the assailant. The superior strength of the beast weakened its intruders resolve, with its own deranged determination to slaughter now an obsession.

Bang! The shot cracked the air, fit to burst the eardrums. A bloodcurdling wail from the dog. Sudden silence, a stink of cordite. Heavy breathing, the drip, drip of the tap.

"Did l get 'un?" Begg croaked his query. Gulping for his breathing to return to near normal, Rolo managed.

"Yeah, you gottun Begg, nearly me too." He stood to inspect a finger bloodied from a stray pellet and pulled the red spotted kerchief from his neck and wrapped it around the injury. The boy lay half-conscious at his feet, the great lump of muscle bone and sinew of the fearsome beast now still, beside him. "Sorry ee's dead" he added.

"That you is it, Rolo? — Well, twere either 'ee or thee. Pah! Never liked the bugger anyways. Alright wiv oi 'o course but a 'orrible bugger all the same" Begg lowered the shotgun. "You remember thit time 'ee got out an' 'ad the cow? Poor sod bled to death. Caused oi no end o' trouble —" he hesitated, "you got someone else there Roly?" His head cocked in the blackbird imitation again. Rolo bent and hauled the groggy boy to his feet by his good shoulder in a firm enough grip to keep him upright with help. Far from being in any state to run anymore, he drowsily looked down at the cause of his near demise as the animal lay lifeless, blood seeping from the fatal, if chanced, wound in its neck.

"Only young Jem 'ere, we was passin' by an' Jem though 'ee saw someone breakin' in didn't us lad?" Rolo lightly shook the boy's collar to warn he should not be contradicted, though the boy was too preoccupied putting his senses together.

"Breakin' in? Wassum wanna break in 'ere for? Oi ain't got nuffin, and what wiv the dog 'ere, ee'd 'ave to be pretty stupid. Thought you'd a known better yourself Roly, 'ere you ain't hurt is 'ee Jem?" Still limp in Rolo's grip, Terry's head spoke on his behalf.

"Ee'll be alright, jest a bit shook up thats all," he rattled the collar some more. "Ah well, we wiz wrong. We'll get rid of 'un an' clean up the mess for 'ee Begg, you carry on wi yer business." Begg turned away to accept the offer then was reminded and dropped his voice conspiratorially.

"Yer, Rolo, I don' 'spose you're 'ad any luck yet wiv a woman fer me?"

"Still workin' on it Begg" Rolo looked at the dead animal. "Honest an' truthful, it might be a bit easier now." Begg was encouraged.

"Well, oi ain't gettin any younger, bit o' company'd be nice. Don' think I'll get another dog though" As they spoke still, the motes of plaster from the shot that hit the wall behind were settling in the air like tiny snowflakes, the surreal calm of conversation after the mayhem went on.

"A bird, a singer. That's what you want, less trouble," Begg was thoughtful at the suggestion.

"A bird, eh? Mmm. See what you mean. Mebbe a Canary or a Linnet. I could even make a cage for un, never tried that. One for the shed as well — Do women like birds Roly?"

"Love 'em Begg, love 'em." Satisfied, and cutting a small smile at the prospect, the blind man began to return through the parlour door as if nothing of any consequence had taken place.

"Begg," Rolo interrupted once more in curiosity. "Why you got a shotgun?" The old man turned again.

"Send a barrel up the chimney after they Jackdaw nest, that clears it. Don't 'alf make yer ears ring though'." Rolo stared after the man in wonderment. His breathing was returning to normal, as had his optimism for living longer after the uproar, and he turned to the slowly recovering boy in his grasp.

"We'll clean this mess up, then you an' I is goin' to 'ave a talk. A long talk." For the first time, Terry managed a weak utterance.

"I ain't got your money," he defended, still sagging in exhaustion.

"Oh I found that alright — 'ventually. This is summat else. What's called 'obson's choice. The only choice you'll get. Now, let me 'ave a look at this shoulder 'an we'll 'ave a chat, or rather, I'll talk an you'll 'ave a listen." He looked at the dog once more, laying like the trophy of a big game hunt. "I think Jem's gonner 'ave to dig a bigger 'ole, bout the size o' the one you dug fer yerself."

CHAPTER TWENTY TWO

It was some two weeks later when Rolo was sat
at the old, cluttered kitchen table at Misserly, slowly
rolling a cigarette with ceremony though with little
concentration, satisfied his plan was coming to fruition.
Clem was in an opposite chair, in recovering spirits,
though still begrudging of recent events. Still too weak
for manual labour, his frustration was evident in
criticism of the transformation. Grace was taking a pair
of kitchen scissors to his hair with no regard to style,
taking random stabs from the thinning locks that had
sprouted during his convalescence, like gathering a posy
from a flower bed. She was humming a random tune. On
seeing the resulting efforts, Rolo had quickly demurred
from the offer of attention to his own growing mop.

"They'm in lower field now, nearly done" he
updated a scowling Clem, tainted with the reluctant
acceptance of Rolo's successful strategy thrashed out at
the very same table. Faced with losing the farm, their
home and their very existence, Clem's back was to the
wall, bitterly accepting the ridiculous scheme Rolo
unveiled was the only option. Still, he was unaware of
the behind-the-scenes manipulation with the ministry,
and had all but given up hope of knowing exactly what

had been going on.

"Well, 'ee won't be 'ere much longer." Rolo was pacifying another of Clem's gripes. "Oi know some people in Nailsea, nice folk, run a garage, repairs an' the like, nuthin' fancy, they be 'appy to take 'im on until we kin' sort it proper." Unrelenting in his grudge against the newcomer, Clem was suspicious of the events that led him to be here at all. The rumble of a car engine distracted their attention. A snip of Clem's lobe made him howl. It pulled into the yard and stopped; two doors slammed. More than one visitor then. They looked quizzically at each other. Clem's scowl blackened. The men rose and opened the black door, Clem holding his ear. Grace preferred the relative security of a view through the kitchen window and was already growing distraught. She saw a black ford popular, whose occupants had gathered at the bottom of the steps and looked up.

"There he is! That's the man! Arrest him at once, constable!" Arthur Bolsover-cox was apoplectic at finding his man here as a bonus to the purpose of his visit, almost hopping in excitement and pointing an accusing finger up at a bemused Rolo. Having resurrected his damning file, he was more keen than ever to see through the compulsory purchase order and be the victor of recent torrid events. The constable, deprived of his lunch break to escort the gentleman here, was not so vehement.

"If you'll calm down sir, and cease from nudging me in the back, I'm sure we can all get to the bottom of this." He turned to the man who had been at his ear all the way from Shapton police station. The desk sergeant had agreed, in order for Arthur to carry out his order he be escorted by the constable, 'for my own safety' as he pleaded. The journey was full of varying accounts of ill deeds that thoroughly confused the hungry policeman.

Rolo helped Clem down the steps with Arthur

taking a half stride back behind the constable for cover, looking nervously at Rolo. As a result of his refusal to enter the house again and Clem's defiance to allow him, all parties, save Grace, who continued her observations from the window humming a tuneless lullaby, gathered either side the bonnet of the popular, Arthur at the constable's side. The crude map of the farm was spread out with Rolo's fat finger drawn across various points of contention while he spoke. His movements were unnoticeably causing his belt buckle to scrape away at the pristine paintwork, while its owner was growing a dangerous shade of purple at the conclusion of his presentation.

"So, there you be, me old drinking companion." Arthur cringed at the slur, Clem and the policeman looked confused.   "If you 'an yer committee would care to inspect, you'll find North fields ploughed an' ready fer seed, five acres to the rhines, likewise ready fer spud in the spring an' east four acre ploughed as recommended in yer report of the requisition order, which I'm sure the committee will now be 'appy to make null an' void when they sees fer theyselves." He stood erect, thumbs in waistcoat pockets as they all looked at Arthur for a response, who gaped while glancing at each man several times.

"B-but — how did —?" He was lost again, and turning a violent red. A fleck of spittle flew across the air as he tried again.   "It's not possible! And there's something else constable, this — this oaf conspired to make me hand over —" he stopped himself.

"What is it, Arthur? What was it you gave me that wouldn't see you in a good light? Pray tell old chap." Rolo leaned forward keenly, with mild amusement at his adversary's suffering.

"Sir?" The policeman offered to the agonised accuser, who was by now suffering his worst case of heartburn ever.

"I am not the criminal here! He is!" He

exploded. It was all going wrong for the man who only minutes earlier was anticipating his finest hour. "This-this scoundrel has deliberately —" he paused again to find a new angle of attack and suddenly remembered.

"The car — yes! — the car! Officer, give him the summons! Ha!" He almost hopped from foot in delirium and nudged the affronted officer heavily, who cleared his throat and turned his attention to Rolo, saying almost reluctantly, "Well sir, as it happens. I do have a matter of police business." He stressed the last two words with a glance at Arthur who was sensing a compensatory triumph. "You are, sir, one Roland Percy, care of this address, subject to prosecution regarding a traffic accident on November twenty eighth of this year." He fished through various pockets before producing a document. "I have to present you with a summons to appear at Bristol magistrates court regarding the same, on the date stated." Rolo readily accepted with good grace and folding it, placed it in his waistcoat pocket.

"To which I will attend in 'cordance with the law" he replied reverently. "Now, if there's nuffin else gentlemen, this man has a farm to run an' would appreciate you waste no more of his valuable time, an' I bid you good day."

"Yeah, piss off!" Clem glowered at Arthur who barked at the constable.

"Well! Is that it? Aren't you going to arrest him?! He's broken the law! Do your job man!" Not appreciating the slight and certainly not another heavy elbow, the policeman sighed with impatience.

"The gentleman has been served his summons and will be dealt with in due course and now, if there's nothing else…" A pencil thick vein that ran from Arthur's right ear to the inside of his stiff, white collar pulsed alarmingly, his face an unhealthy shade of purple by now.

"Careful Arthur" Rolo said, "if you was a boiler, we'd 'ave to take a step back frum the danger of flying rivets!"

"You-You've not heard the last of this, hear me?" Came the desperate last riposte. The map, uncooperating in failing to fold into its normal creases was scrunched angrily and thrown into the car, the door slammed, and the engine started. Almost too late, the constable scrambled to the passenger door for his lift, albeit he had not presented himself in a good light to Bolsover-Cox, and were it not for his hunger for dinner, wondered that a long walk back to the station would be preferable. The car departed with an irate crunching of gears and scattering hens with Clem and Rolo looking on. Clem was in a rare high mood, albeit there were huge gaps in his understanding of the meeting. With Rolo's help they mounted the steps to be greeted by a tearful looking Grace, upset at the raised voices. She looked at Rolo beseechingly, who put a comforting arm around her shoulder.

"S'alright Gracie girl, s'alright. Tell 'ee what, you get a jug warmin' an' we'll 'ave a toast." His avuncular eyes smiled.

"You were late this mornin'," Terry accused his co-worker who returned with an increasingly familiar contortion of a smile.

"'ad to go trappin' early" he explained over the engine noise. "It's Mr Begg, ee wants all I can get. Ee's sellin' 'em in the cages ee's makin' an' payin' me 'alf a crown each — want me to 'ave a go now" For once Terry was keen to dismount the makeshift pull tractor, feeling the stiffness in his shoulder still, less than pleased to hear Begg's name mentioned again. More than once he'd cursed Jem for not forewarning him of the dog. "But I didn't know, honest, all 'ee ever said was keep away from the 'ouse."was his only offer of defence.

Eagerly, Jem climbed aboard the strange contraption for his turn at the wheel, a simple but odd-looking affair, Terry had worked tirelessly with overseeing from Rolo, to fashion it into the purpose Will had intended all those years ago. The boys tinkering hadn't gone unnoticed by Rolo who put him to good use to finish the project he'd covertly found an interest in. The plough share was duly attached once straightened, and even allowed for a seed drill to be towed. It had no bodywork as such, the chassis completed with its engine mounted on a steel plate, the great steel wheel spikes bit heavily into the soil, and the single seat still atop an extended rod from its base. The robust, if quirky vehicle was capable of everything. Rolo had specified with Terry's latent talent for mechanics, which the boy was to discover came easily and for the first time in his life, gratifying.

On completion, the boys had spent hours in the fields learning the techniques of the machine's abilities and limitations. How pleasing it was to see the curved blade cut into the green swathe, and magically turn it over into a rich, brown sod behind them, although less than perfectly straight.

By trial and error, they learned the fuel mix, the needy repairs, the comfort of an inventive spring seat to ease vibration, and commonly, each other's reluctance to give up their turn on the new wonder.

A few more days and Terry's part of the agreement would be done. Though he never really understood the urgency to make the contrivance operational, the bargain explained to him did seem pleasing. The prospect of another 'evacuation' nearer to urbanity and the discovery of his aptness for mechanics, had brought a focus on the future that for once gave him a newfound buoyancy, tempered as it was by the requirement to work closely with Jem and his slow-witted ways.

There had been a meeting of sorts between the adults, with Rolo as instigator, mediator and peacekeeper. Voices were raised, no louder than that of Clem's, whose vehement objections could be heard across the yard. For her part, Grace in one of her more lucid moments, berated her brother in failing to address the precariousness of their plight, though she was still confused as to the newcomer and his purpose at the farm. Nevertheless, she was happy to feed him, wash and re-adjust his clothes, and to provide hot water for a series of much needed baths. Exposed to the Bottle clan as he had been, Terry still favoured his own company when possible, and still insisted on sleeping in the pig barn, as much as to keep out of Clem's way as anything, who continued to eye him suspiciously. Having to bitterly concede to the boy having access to the workshop, his sourness was evident.

Jem was relieved his ordeal was over. The deceit had eaten away at him and now he could indulge in Terry's company openly and work together as he always intended. He understood fully this was to be a temporary arrangement and soon the boy would be gone, but the experience of labouring in the fields and finding amity with a peer gave him a new confidence. Terry would never settle here, he knew. But there would be others just as Rolo had said. There was a new urgency about the farm with the preparing of the soil for planting and many hands would be needed. Change was on its way.

CHAPTER TWENTY THREE

"S-So you are in fact an itinerant, Mr Percy?"
The insinuation from the magistrate was not lost on his
fellows, who looked down from a highly polished
walnut-fronted bench and regal looking leather-bound
chairs. The whole room was a study of carpentry skills
with hardwood lacquered in plinths, cornices, tenons and
mitres, all lovingly polished to a fine sheen. A plump
woman of middle age in a feathered hat and stole, sat
one side of the central figure, a serious, slightly
effeminate looking young man whose stutter brought on
a blush of colour to his thin face with the effort. To his
other side slumbered an elderly gentleman, who
appeared to take little part in proceedings.

Though the dock of the accused was in fact only
marginally lower in height than the bench, its elevating
superiority was enough to lend an intimidating presence
across the musty room. A smattering of public faces had
taken shelter from the cold and taken up seating, all
unrecognisable to Rolo except that of one Arthur
Bolsover-Cox who sat alone at the front row, hat resting
on his lap, taking an avid interest in the proceedings. The
magistrate's observation gave him a triumphant smirk to

which he turned to his adversary for his response.

"Not at all sir, I do 'ave a 'ome" Rolo stated flatly.

"B-but no address." The accuser turned to his aides in condemnation of the fact.

"Several, sir." Contradicted the man dressed in his familiar waistcoat and collarless shirt, though as a concession to his surroundings had removed his hat. In truth, he did resemble the allegation.

"And would they be on wheels too?" A murmur of giggles from the room, Bolsover-Cox looking more pleased with events as each moment passed. The young man had seemed to take delight in besmirching Rolo's character from the beginning, and although he had pleaded guilty as he had promised from the outset, had little doubt of the bench's hostility. There were occasional glances between the magistrate and Arthur, that didn't go unnoticed by a bemused Rolo, again a cause for concern. But here he was, ready to accept the punishment for his actions and the sooner it was concluded, the sooner he could get on with his day. He didn't have long to wait. The bench had put their collective head together and whispered in hushed tones, the two outsiders seeming to be on nodding terms to the leading young man.

"Mr Percy," he looked up finally.   "W-wilful driving under the influence simply cannot be tolerated. The country is in d-desperate times and you see fit to indulge in your pleasures with no regard to life or p-property. However, I see no benefit in a custodial sentence as fit and able m-men are premium to the country's needs. I will order that you enrol in his m-majesty's service. You will report to the army recruitment office in B-Bayford road tomorrow morning, accompanied by an officer of the law. In the interim you will be held in custody overnight at the p-police cells here." Rolo was led away stunned. Arthur Bolsover-Cox beamed.

The warming sun of early April shone through thin flecks of white cirrus cloud, the busyness of the new season evident below. Larks were rising in the clean morning air, butterflies chased each other above bursting vegetation like they were attached by a small string. The vivid verdant was a palette of every shade of the dominating hues imaginable, the lime and lemon greens of sprouting willows, the brown and black greens of filling hedgerows, bottle greens, pea greens and sea greens, constantly changing their shades as they flourished.

The seeding potatoes had been planted at Misserly and were poking their emerald green shoots through the soil. Winter planted cabbages and kale lay ready for harvest in neat rows, their purplish green crinkled wraps clutched around the meaty hearts. Swathes of lush grasses for hay keep rippled in the breeze, the cattle turned out and enjoying the first sweet taste of lush grass of the year.

Clem had tended to a calf in the warming barn with a split hoof. Moreover, these days he managed fewer challenging tasks about the farm, before his breathing became laboured and he was forced to retire again. Cantankerous as he still was, his begrudging acknowledgement of the breathing of new life about the farm gave some peace from his demons, even to the point of an occasional word of encouragement to Jem.

"Not like that, George!" Jem reprimanded the boy. "Yer wastin' far too much. Now watch an' oi'll show 'ee one more time!" Feigning exasperation with a heavy sigh, Jem took over the knife and bent astride a row of spring cabbages. Deftly he cut through the thick stalk and rolled the cabbage clear.

"Tell 'ee what, I'll cut an' you load" he ordered the novice, "sometimes I wunder if it's worf payin' 'ee" he grumbled. George was suitably chastened.

"Sorry Jem, I'll learn it I will" he promised. Jem

stood upright and looked at the boy, some two years younger than himself. His first recruit from the village was showing varying degrees of ability, though there was no doubting his enthusiasm and perhaps he was a little harsh.

"S'alright George, t' be honest an' truthful I'm still learnin' meself. We'll finish this row and then move they cattle across to four acre. That'll do us fer today. Still reckon yer brother'll come tomorror to 'elp wiv the kale?" George nodded.

"He'll be 'ere Jem, 'ee likes it. Can I see the birds later? Can I?"

Jem stroked his chin as though the wisdom of the ages were upon him.

"Mmm, mebbe later. If us get time we might go out wiv the trap, I'll show 'ee 'ow t' catch em."

The End.

CAN I ASK A FAVOUR?

If you enjoyed this book, found it useful or otherwise, I would really appreciate it if you would post a short review on Amazon. I read all the reviews personally, so that I can continually write what people are wanting.

Thank you for taking the time to read this book and thank you for your support!

Made in the USA
Columbia, SC
04 June 2021